The Computer Game Murder

Milton Dank & Gloria Dank

The Computer Game Murder

Milton Dank & Gloria Dank

Delacorte Press/New York

Published by
Delacorte Press
1 Dag Hammarskjold Plaza
New York, N.Y. 10017

MANUFACTURED IN THE UNITED STATES OF AMERICA

FIRST PRINTING

Library of Congress Cataloging in Publication Data
Dank, Milton [date of birth].
The computer game murder.
(A Galaxy Gang mystery)
Summary: When thirteen-year-old Larry receives a message on his computer screen during a game, indicating his playing partner is in trouble, a long and dangerous investigation involving the Galaxy Gang begins.
1. Children's stories, American. [1. Computers—Fiction. 2. Mystery and detective stories] I. Dank, Gloria. II. Title.
PZ7.D228Cod 1985 [Fic]
ISBN 0-385-29411-5
Library of Congress Catalog Card Number: 85-1650

To George Badra, with our love

1

□ WHAT IS THE NAME OF THE ALIEN HIT MAN WHO CON-
FRONTS HAN SOLO IN THE CANTINA SCENE IN "STAR
WARS"?

The greenish message danced across the computer
screen as Larry Strauss groaned. *Star Wars!* He had
seen it on TV only last week, the second rerun this
year. He remembered the scene perfectly: the alien
with the high, spiny skull and long snout, one of
Jabba the Hutt's henchmen, aiming his weapon at
Han Solo. The strange-looking crowd in the dimly lit
cantina carefully paying no attention—then *Boom!* as
Solo blasted the would-be killer.

Larry could almost see the grin on the face of his
unknown opponent. Real names were never used in
this computer game. Some of the players were using
their employers' computers during lunch and after
office hours. They preferred high-sounding names

like "Fearless Phone," "The Grand Inquisitor," or "Moby Disk." Larry was "Mr. Chips" and he always signed off with "Good-bye—Mr. Chips." He was not sure that all of his opponents had read the book or seen the picture, but he liked the literary touch.

Greeno? No, that wasn't it, although he may well have been green. Larry looked at the clock on the basement wall above his computer workbench. By the rules he had to answer in two minutes or concede. There were seventy seconds left.

Except for the hum of the furnace, it was quiet in the basement. His parents had just returned from a social meeting at the synagogue, where Larry's father, Rabbi David Strauss, had spoken on modern marriage. Larry had been invited but had pleaded extreme youth and an inability to face the problems of matrimony. His mother had smiled, but his father had warned against spending too much time in the basement staring at the monitor screen. "You'll need glasses before you're fifteen," Rabbi Strauss had complained, "and will talk only in computerese."

Forty seconds . . . no hope. There was a copy of *Star Wars* upstairs under his bed, but that would be cheating. Larry slapped the desk in frustration as the second hand of the clock swept on. Sphinx would know the answer for sure. The rest of the Galaxy Gang probably knew it too. Diggy, Chessie, Bobbie—even Tilo, who had arrived in Philadelphia from Vietnam only two years ago.

Larry hated to lose. More than once Chessie had

2

told him that this competitive streak was wrong among friends. "Save it for school," she had told him. "There's nothing wrong with being number one in your class, but don't try it on us. The Galaxy Gang works together. You know more about electronic gadgets than the rest of us, but don't try to beat Sphinx in science or math—or Diggy in history."

TIME'S UP flashed on the screen. Desperate, Larry took a wild guess. REGO, he typed with a sinking heart, knowing he was wrong even before his fingers touched the keyboard.

WRONG! his opponent gloated. IT'S GREEDO AND I MOVE TO RED SQUARE FOUR. A picture of the playing board appeared on the screen and Larry watched as his opponent's marker moved forward. This guy is good, Larry thought miserably. Two more questions that I can't answer and he'll win again. This was the third game he had played against "The Squire" and he had yet to win one. Larry opened the notebook in which he kept lists of questions for the game. Red square meant a science question. Larry ran down the list and came to one that Sphinx had suggested only yesterday. He typed:

FOR WHAT WORK WAS ALBERT EINSTEIN GIVEN THE NOBEL PRIZE?

Larry grinned gleefully as the screen stayed blank. The Squire was puzzled, suspecting a trap, and he was right. Ninety seconds passed before he hesitantly tapped out his answer, the obvious one: RELATIVITY.

WRONG! IT WAS FOR EXPLAINING THE PHOTOELECTRIC

3

EFFECT AND PROVING THAT LIGHT COULD ACT AS A PARTI-
CLE.

Thank you, Sphinx, Larry breathed gratefully.
That may be the break I need. He sat back in his
chair and waited for the next question. It never came.

Suddenly a line of GS . . . GS . . . GS . . . flashed
across the screen, then nothing. "Game suspended."
Something had happened—maybe The Squire's boss
had walked in or his wife or someone had called him.
Anyway, it was now on hold until some future time.
Larry pressed the buttons that put the game onto a
disk. Then he labeled it, and put the disk into a
drawer.

He felt cheated. True, he was behind right now,
but he had been elated by the success of his last question. With a little luck he might have edged The
Squire with some snappy answers and a few more
tough questions. Now he would have to wait.

In his notebook were the telephone numbers of a
dozen other players. He tried Moby Disk, but there
was no answer. "Captain Gallant" said he was too
busy doing his father's income tax. The next three
numbers did not reply and Larry was almost ready to
quit. Only the idea of spending a Sunday afternoon
doing homework or cleaning up his room kept him
dialing. He knew that the rest of the Galaxy Gang
would not be available until after dinner, so it was
the game or utter boredom.

He dialed again. Nothing. Then he saw that the
next number was "Peter Pan," and his heart jumped.

Please, he prayed silently, let her be there and free to play.

"Peter Pan" was a thirteen-year-old boy's secret dream: an older woman. Six weeks ago she had phoned in for the first time. Larry's code name and telephone number were on the bulletin board of a local computer parts store, a hangout for all the computer enthusiasts looking for secondhand components and free technical advice. Andy Willis, who ran the store, was a street-smart computer genius of twenty-one. He ran the store like a club, letting anyone with a real interest in the latest computer technology read all the new magazines or just talk. When Larry had asked him if he had met Peter Pan, Andy had nodded and whispered, "She's really something."

It took Larry fifteen minutes to find out that Peter Pan was more than just an attractive young woman . . . "twenty-two, maybe twenty-three" . . . and that she was a computer programmer in a stockbroker's office. Andy had tried desperately to get her name and phone number, but she had laughingly refused. "She's very sharp on software," Andy said thoughtfully, "and knows a lot about new systems. I explained the game to her and gave her my number, but she never called. I saw her copying something from the bulletin board and she bought a manual on the ZR-10. That's all I know 'cause she never came back."

"Didn't you get her name and address on the sales slip?"

"Yeah. Peter Pan from Shangri-la. Big deal. Who won the game?"

Larry quickly interested himself in a magazine and then left without the answer to his question. Peter Pan had swept the game board not once but twice. She had an amazing store of information on four of the six subjects that went into the game. Time and again she had answered correctly some of the toughest questions on literature, history, music, and films. Her only weaknesses had been in current events and geography. By the time Larry had found her weak spots, she was too far ahead to be caught.

"I don't think I tried very hard," Larry confided to Chessie. He was still irked by what had been said about his competitive streak and was trying to prove it was not true. "But it was sure fun to play the game with her."

"And that's not the only game you'd like to play with her," Chessie had said with a mischievous grin. "Larry, you're a hopeless romantic. And on top of that you usually want to win. What a combination."

It's true, Larry thought. I picked questions about love stories, books like *Wuthering Heights* and *Jane Eyre*. And romantic spots like Paris and Venice.

THIS IS PETER PAN. WHO IS CALLING? The message appeared on the screen and Larry swallowed hard.

MR. CHIPS CALLING. HELLO, PETER PAN. ARE YOU READY FOR ANOTHER MATCH?

There was a moment's hesitation before the next

message. I'D LOVE TO, CHIPS, BUT I HAVE THIS BIG RUSH JOB TO FINISH.

PLEASE, Larry pleaded, JUST A HALF HOUR. I WANT TO TRY A NEW STRATEGY.

Peter Pan thought this over, then typed: OKAY, BUT ONLY A HALF HOUR. YOU BEGIN.

Quickly consulting his notebook, Larry typed: WHO WAS HELOISE'S LOVER? He blushed as he typed. This was the first time he had ever used the word *lover* or *love* or anything like that. He wondered if Peter Pan would guess how he felt. In a strange way, he hoped that she would. A hopeless romantic, Chessie had said. Certainly a modern one, Larry thought, using a computer to send love notes.

The answer was quick. ABELARD. I DIDN'T KNOW THAT YOU KNEW THAT ONE. Larry flushed again. She thinks I'm a kid, a hacker but too young. Then he became angry. I'll show her.

He waited for her question. Usually Peter Pan worked very quickly, never hesitating in picking a question, but now for some reason the screen remained blank.

STAND BY, MR. CHIPS. I THINK I HEAR SOMEONE OUTSIDE. Larry groaned. Another interruption. Now she would terminate. He waited impatiently, shifting about on the kitchen chair that he found most comfortable for long hours in front of the computer. Five minutes passed and Peter Pan was still silent. Larry opened a computer magazine and began to read the ads.

He was reading about a new phone patch system when out of the corner of his eye, he saw a message appear on the screen. It took him a while to grasp what he was reading. No message like this had ever appeared before during a game. CHIPS, I'M SCARED. HELP ME.

Puzzled, Larry could only stare at the screen. Was this some sort of joke? Was Peter Pan making fun of him? SCARED OF WHAT? WHAT'S GOING ON THERE?

The screen remained blank. Larry typed the message again, adding PLEASE ANSWER. No response. Larry's mouth was dry and he felt a vein pulsing on his right temple. What had happened to Peter Pan? Had she fallen and hurt herself? No, she had said she was scared, not hurt. Someone must have broken into her room and frightened her.

When the answer came, it was short and broken. IT'S ON THE D . . . Then there was a click from the phone as the connection was cut. Larry dialed again, but there was only a busy signal. What's going on? he wondered. First she sounds frightened and wants help, then she signs off and is calling someone else.

He kept trying the number every few minutes, but it was still busy. Either Peter Pan was having a long conversation with someone or the telephone was off the hook. Larry thought of calling the police, but what could he tell them? Some strange girl whose address he did not know had typed a message on his computer that she was scared and wanted help. He could imagine what Sergeant Gauss would think of

8

that! The sergeant had been involved in several of the Galaxy Gang's adventures and he had never been very happy with what he called their "scatterbrained attitude toward danger." No, the best thing to do was wait and try to reach Peter Pan later tonight or tomorrow.

Switching off his computer, Larry cleaned the table and covered his equipment. He was still nervous and unhappy about what had happened, but more puzzled than anything. There was probably a simple explanation, although it certainly escaped him right now. He turned off the light and left the basement. Behind him, he heard the furnace click on and the *whoosh* of the flames. Cold outside, he thought absentmindedly.

"All done, dear?" his mother asked as he came up the cellar stairs into the kitchen. He tried to smile, but his lips refused to move. He hurried out of the kitchen to keep his mother from seeing his strained expression. The door to his father's study was closed and he could hear the tapping of a typewriter. That meant his father was either writing a sermon or a scholarly paper and was not to be disturbed unless the house caught fire. Even then the Strauss family would have hesitated to disturb the rabbi until the flames threatened the study.

As soon as he entered his bedroom Larry saw that his mother had cleaned it in his absence. The pile of electronics magazines that had been scattered on the bed were now neatly piled in a corner and all his

books were back on the shelves. To make a point, his mother had left one dirty sock hanging from the lamp cord, where it turned slowly in the breeze from the half-open window. Larry untied the sock and threw it into the hamper. Shivering, he shut the window and drew the shade against the cold night. What a depressing day, he thought. Why had Peter Pan shut him off like that?

He went across the hall to his parents' bedroom and picked up the telephone. Diggy, he knew, was visiting relatives, and Chessie and Bobbie were at an art show, but Sphinx might be at home. He dialed and at the fifth ring a sleepy voice said, "Osgood residence. They're all out. Sorry, but disappointment builds character."

"Sphinx, it's Larry. I have to talk to you about something that just happened." Sphinx groaned and there was the sound of a cup hitting a dish and then the rush of running water.

"This better be important. You just interrupted a gourmet meal—bananas with yogurt, crushed walnuts, and bread crumbs."

"Forgive me while I fight back a sudden wave of nausea," Larry said.

"What's up?"

Quickly Larry told him of the strange messages he had just received from Peter Pan. As the story came out he felt more and more foolish for getting so alarmed, and he ended by mumbling several possible explanations for why the game had ended so

abruptly. Sphinx agreed. "Try her later," he suggested, "maybe tomorrow. I'm sure you'll contact her and she'll have a good reason for what she did. Maybe you were cut off accidentally. . . ."

"Maybe, but I doubt it. She certainly was scared and was trying to tell me something. And when I tried her number again, there was a busy signal, as if someone was using the phone."

Sphinx yawned. This was not his type of puzzle. Why people did what they did—especially women— was a mystery that math and physics could not solve. He reminded Larry of the times that Chessie and Bobbie had acted strangely—"as far as we could see, anyway, but they always had this weird logic for what they had done."

Larry agreed that the best thing was to wait and try to contact Peter Pan later. When he hung up, he was still vaguely dissatisfied. In the back of his mind there was a lurking fear that something terrible had happened and he was helpless to do anything about it. He tried Tilo's number, but there was no answer.

Larry turned on the shortwave radio set he had built into the headboard of his bed. He liked to listen to all the foreign broadcasts, dozens of languages that he could not understand. Just the sound of someone speaking French or Spanish soothed him. He listened for a while to what seemed to be a play from Paris, then switched to the BBC news from London. In beautifully precise tones, the announcer was heralding a victory for England in cricket. Larry turned to a station that was playing Mozart, stretched out on the bed, and shut his eyes.

CHIPS, I'M SCARED. HELP ME. Scared of what? That didn't sound like she was interrupted by someone walking in and finding her using the computer to play the game. I THINK I HEAR SOMEONE OUTSIDE. Why was she so frightened of being caught? Did she think she would be fired? IT'S ON THE D . . ." The desk? What was on the desk?

Finally, Larry could not stand the tension of not knowing. He got up and went down to the basement. Turning on the computer, he picked up the phone and dialed Peter Pan. For a long time he heard it ringing, but there was no answer. He called the operator and asked her to check if the phone was in order. It was.

"Can you tell me the address at which this phone is located?" Larry asked.

"Sorry," the operator said firmly. "We are not allowed to give that information." *Click.*

He sat staring at the blank screen, trying to still the pounding of his heart. There was no logic to it. There were probably a dozen good explanations for what had happened, but Larry could not get rid of the thought that something terrible had happened to Peter Pan.

He was still sitting silent and motionless when his mother called him up for dinner. He sat moodily through the meal, saying little and picking at his food. His mother asked if he was well, but he just mumbled something about a test in school.

That night he had a hard time getting to sleep. That Peter Pan was in trouble was clear to him, but what sort of trouble and what could he do about it? Finally, exhausted, he fell into a fitful doze.

The nightmare was terrible. Peter Pan was flying through space and calling for help. Behind her, Jabba the Hutt and Darth Vader were in hot pursuit, firing laser guns. Larry was trying to intercept the two villains, but he found he could not move. He struggled and cried out as he watched them descending on her.

When the alarm clock woke him, he found that he was twisted up in his bedclothes and bathed in perspiration.

2

☐ "Larry!" Chessie whispered. "What's wrong? You look like you haven't slept for a week."

In front of her, Diggy turned and stared. Larry was slumped at his desk, his face puffy-white with red-rimmed eyes. He was yawning uncontrollably and the pencil kept falling out of his hand. In the front of the class, Mrs. Evans, the history teacher, was peering over her glasses at him.

"Leave me alone," Larry mumbled. His chin dropped down on his chest and his lower lip trembled. Sphinx looked over at Chessie and shook his head. To divert the teacher's attention, he raised his hand and asked a trivial question. With a sigh, Mrs. Evans answered, but Sphinx kept the conversation going until the bell rang. Then the Galaxy Gang gathered around Larry and walked him out of the classroom.

14

In the lavatory, Diggy and Sphinx held Larry's head under the cold water despite his violent protests. "Wake up," Diggy said, "before one of our teachers spots you and thinks you're high on something." Larry spat water and tried to talk, but his two friends firmly plunged his face down into the basin and splashed the icy water over the back of his neck. Larry jumped as the water trickled down his back. "Okay," he sputtered. "Stop it, already. I'm awake."

Tilo came in with a towel from the gym and they dried Larry off briskly. As Larry combed his hair unsteadily, Sphinx told Diggy and Tilo the story of Peter Pan and the strange doings of last night.

"You mean you let yourself get into this condition over something that probably has a simple explanation?" Diggy asked. "Some girl can't finish playing the game with you and you dream up some terrible danger to her. Larry, you're hopeless."

"Easy, Diggy," Sphinx put in. "He feels bad enough as it is. Besides, it sure sounds funny the way she cut off."

"Okay," Diggy backtracked. "Let's get to class. We can talk about this more at lunch." Larry shook his head to clear it and started to say something, then tightened his lips. As they stepped out into the crowded corridor, Mrs. Evans was standing in front of the faculty lounge with the assistant principal. They looked thoughtfully at the four boys as they passed. Sphinx smiled and would have bowed, but Diggy jabbed him in the ribs with an elbow.

The cafeteria was bedlam. Hundreds of conversations, giggles, groans, and shouts for quiet. The gang found a 'table at the back and isolated themselves from the waves of noise. It was a trick they had when there was a serious problem to discuss. Huddled around Larry, who was drooped over his tray, they talked quietly, oblivious to their surroundings. Chessie and Bobbie had been told the strange story of Peter Pan and the interrupted game.

"Diggy's right," Bobbie said. "This is all a fuss over nothing. So she couldn't—or didn't want to—finish the game, that's no reason to lose sleep. You've been seeing too many horror movies, Larry." She looked with distaste at her tuna fish sandwich.

Chessie watched Larry struggle with his food and said nothing. When Larry caught her stare and smiled, she looked away, pretending to be watching two boys balancing their trays on their heads. She thought she knew why Larry was so upset and she was jealous. Not that she felt for Larry what she felt for Diggy, but Peter Pan was an interloper, a stranger who was intruding into the tightly knit gang. Unlike Bobbie, Chessie Morelli was a romantic in the traditional Italian style. Love stories made her weep, but not when a good friend fell for an older woman he'd never seen. That, she felt, was vaguely disloyal.

Tilo had a practical suggestion. "Go to the police. They will find out where this woman lives and if she is okay."

16

Sphinx swallowed a bite of his sandwich, then shook his head. "Won't help," he said. "Sergeant Gauss would throw Larry out in a flash. What kind of story is that? I'm playing a game on the computer with some girl . . ."

"Woman!" Bobbie snarled.

Sphinx flinched as if hit. "Woman," he corrected himself, "who suddenly says she is hearing things, that she's afraid, and then cuts off. Where's the crime?"

Sergeant Gauss worked out of the Pine Street police station and had been involved—to his constant regret—in several of the Galaxy Gang's adventures. A friend of Chessie's family, he was always warning the teenagers about getting into trouble. In his gruff way he tried to watch over the gang and to make certain that they did not get involved in anything they could not handle.

"What about the judge?" Diggy asked. Judge Jarrell, a widower retired from the courts, was a good friend whose garage served as the gang's clubhouse. Like Sergeant Gauss, he tried to guide the youngsters, advise them on the fine points of the law, and keep them out of trouble.

"Same thing," Sphinx said. "He'd call Sergeant Gauss and the two of them would say that nothing can be done without evidence that there's been a crime. Grown-ups are sticky about things like that: no evidence, no crime, and therefore no investigation. Habeas corpus." Sphinx grinned triumphantly as he saw the blank stares of his friends. "Produce the body or don't bother us with your suspicions."

" 'If the law says that,' " Larry said miserably, " 'then the law is an ass.' " He tried to remember who had first said that but could not come up with a name. His friends looked at him sympathetically. Quotes were Larry's strong point. He could usually be depended on to come up with something appropriate for any occasion.

They finished their lunch almost in silence. Bobbie started to talk about the art show she and Chessie had seen, but it seemed like idle chatter in the face of Larry's anxiety. The noise in the cafeteria now intruded on their conversation and they did not linger over their food. Long before the bell rang, they had left the lunchroom and dispersed to their next class.

For the rest of the afternoon Larry sat in class without really being present. He heard nothing of what his teachers were saying. When the school day ended, he slipped out by the gym entrance to avoid running into any of the gang. Cutting across the playing field, he walked quickly to Willis's "Hackers' Heaven," on Monroe Street. The store was a narrow three-story brick building squeezed in between a fish market ("Fresh catch every day") and a camera store whose windows were covered with blaring signs of big discounts.

Andy Willis was unpacking some new merchandise at the rear of the store when Larry entered. He looked up, smiled, and waved a handful of crushed paper. Andy's policy was never to approach one of his customers until they asked for his help, so Larry was able to check the bulletin board undisturbed. There were the usual "for sale" ads offering used components and systems. Someone was starting a class in advanced programming. Someone else was looking for parts for an obsolete computer. The board was cluttered with slips of papers, some typed, some handwritten. There was nothing from Peter Pan.

Larry pretended to browse through the magazines on the rack near the door, then walked nonchalantly to the back where Andy was working. "Hi," he said. "Anything new on that IBM home job?"

"September was the announced date," Andy replied, "but it won't get into the stores until December at the latest. If you're thinking of buying one, I can quote you a good price." They both laughed at the idea of Larry purchasing a five thousand dollar computer.

"No, thanks. I was asking for a friend of mine who is interested—if it's as good as the publicity says." Larry leaned on the counter and watched Willis empty a carton. Trying to keep his voice calm, he said, "By the way, have you seen that girl from Shangri-la, what's her name?"

Andy dusted off a monitor before answering. He had caught the tremor in Larry's voice. "Yeh, she came in Saturday just before closing and bought a box of nine-inch floppies. Said something about having an important job to do this weekend—last weekend, I mean. She seemed kind of excited about it, all breathless and red in the face. She must have been running to get here before we closed."

"Did she say what kind of job?"

"Nope. And the name was still Peter Pan, in case you were about to ask." Andy grinned. "What's going on between you two? Don't tell me a thirteen-year-old hacker is doing better with this girl than I am. My ego won't take it."

For a split second Larry considered telling Andy of the mysterious messages. Then he turned red, thinking of the ribbing he would get if it really was nothing. He mumbled something about an interrupted game and hurried out of the store. Better not let too many people know what's going on, he thought.

Suddenly he stopped dead and slapped his forehead in disgust. Of course, she works for a stockbroker! She was probably working in the office on Sunday— unless she has a terminal at home. His heart racing, Larry turned on South Street and hurried to the public library. The Philadelphia classified telephone directory was on the shelf with directories from all the nearby suburban towns. There were three long columns of "Stock and Bond Brokers" and Larry carefully checked the telephone numbers. None matched the number Peter Pan had given him. One by one he pulled the suburban books off the shelf and checked them, too. Nothing matched.

Either it's an unlisted number or she works at

home, Larry thought. In either case I can't find her—unless she answers the phone.

From the library to his home was eight blocks and Larry ran most of the way. His mother was on the upstairs phone arranging a tennis match when he arrived and he sat impatiently in the basement workshop until she finished. He dialed Peter Pan's number with trembling fingers.

Larry gasped as someone picked up the phone! "Army recruiting. Corporal Williams speaking," a gruff voice said.

"Sorry, sir," Larry said weakly. "Wrong number." Army recruiting—if he didn't snap out of this depression soon, he'd end up in a straitjacket, not army green. He dialed again, this time carefully. There was a long wait, then a recorded voice said, "The number you have dialed, 555-2041, has been disconnected."

He sat for a long time staring at the phone but seeing nothing. His fingers were trembling and there was a sharp pain between his eyes. He tried to think, but everything was confused and made no sense. Why had Peter Pan disconnected her phone? Had she had the number changed so she would not be bothered by hackers like Larry, or was there some other reason?

All he could understand was that his last chance to reach her had disappeared.

For the rest of the week, Larry was unable to shake the idea that something was terribly wrong. In class, he sat without hearing and failed to respond when his name was called. Finally, one of his teachers sent him to the school psychologist. To the gently probing questions, Larry answered with noncommittal, often irrelevant replies. He did not expect a grown-up to understand that what he was suffering from was a kind of premonition.

To his worried friends in the gang, he showed an unaccountable anger and hurt. When they approached him and tried to humor him, he responded with sarcasm and bitterness. For the first time he felt that the gang had let him down. He had expected them to understand his fears and to help—how, he did not know, since he could not help himself. The Galaxy Gang was important to him. They were the brothers and sisters he did not have, and they had let him down. Even Tilo, the gentlest soul of all, had gotten the sharp edge of Larry's tongue.

Diggy went looking for Chessie on Friday afternoon during the study hall period. Sliding into a seat next to her, he whispered, "Chess, we've got to do something about Larry."

Chessie put a marker into her textbook and closed it. "Not *about* Larry, do something *for* Larry. He thinks we let him down—and we did."

Diggy flushed. "Gosh, what were we supposed to do? Produce Peter Pan out of thin air and prove that she was okay? Aren't there enough nerds around to play the game with Larry? Why such a big deal about someone he's never seen?" He slumped down in the seat, his face grim.

"You men!" Chessie whispered disdainfully. "You can't see past your nose. Do you think that Larry has gotten himself into this state just because he lost another hacker who plays the game?"

"What else?"

"Larry may be an electronic whiz with a soldering iron in one hand and a schematic in the other to you, but deep down where it counts he's a romantic, full of wonderful poetry—"

"That he steals from a book of quotations." Diggy ducked as Chessie swung her book at his head. In front of the room, a monitor looked up and made a warning sound.

Diggy leaned over and whispered, "Are you trying to tell me that Larry is in love with a woman he's never seen? Come off it, Chess. Why, she could be sixty!"

"I didn't say he was in love. Maybe he is, although I don't think so. Larry sees Peter Pan as young, pretty, and in trouble. Don't you ever dream of yourself as a knight in shining armor rescuing a beautiful lady from a dragon?"

"Kid stuff," Diggy said scornfully.

Chessie's voice turned icy. "There are times, Digby Caldwell, when I wonder why I put up with you. You know what you are? You're a . . . a . . . a philistine!"

23

Not certain what a philistine was, but alarmed by the angry look in Chessie's eyes, Diggy retreated rapidly. "Gee, Chess, it's just that I'm worried about Larry and the way he's acting. A couple more weeks like this and the gang will fall apart."

Refusing to be mollified, Chessie picked up her books and pushed her way past Diggy to the aisle. On the way she managed to step hard on his foot. Diggy groaned, then quickly smiled as the monitor stood up to glare at him. What was Chessie so sore about? And wasn't Goliath a Philistine? What did that have to do with Larry?

There are times, Francesca Morelli, he thought savagely, when you don't make sense.

Just before dinner, Diggy was sitting cross-legged on the floor in front of the television set. His parents allowed him to watch the reruns of *M*A*S*H*, since he insisted that the Korean War was history and he was writing a school paper on it. His mother had been very skeptical, but his father, a lieutenant commander in the U.S. Navy, still hoped that his son would apply to the Naval Academy someday. This interest in things military seemed like a good sign to Commander Caldwell.

Actually, Diggy was finding it hard to follow the antics of Hawkeye and Trapper as they made Major Frank Burns's life miserable. Shortly after Chessie had stalked out of the study hall, Diggy had gone to the library and checked the dictionary. Now he was steaming. The definition was burned in his mind and he could not forget it. Philistine: a crass, prosaic, often priggish individual guided by material rather than artistic or intellectual values.

Hawkeye and Trapper, dressed in gorilla suits, were picking imaginary fleas off each other, but Diggy was not amused. From the kitchen came delicious smells as his mother prepared dinner, but even that failed to soothe him. "Crass, huh," he muttered, "priggish even. What am I supposed to do? Put on a suit of armor and fight dragons too?"

He was still nursing his hurt feelings when the six o'clock news came on. Deep in plotting his revenge, he barely heard the voice of the announcer: "A fire in a North Philadelphia boardinghouse cost the life of an elderly man early this morning. . . . The Department of Labor announced today that food prices had risen for the third month in a row. . . . The police are investigating the disappearance of a young woman in center city. Patricia Penndell was last seen . . . Mike Schmidt broke open the ball game this afternoon with one of his patented home runs, leading the Phillies to a five-to-four victory over the . . . And now the weather . . ."

"Diggy," his mother called, "turn off the television and set the table, please." Diggy switched off the set, got to his feet, and shuffled into the kitchen. As he loaded a tray with napkins and silverware, he threw a sideways glance at his mother.

"Something on your mind?" his mother asked.

Diggy swallowed hard, then blurted out, "Chessie says I'm a philistine. That means I'm crass and—"

"I know what the word means," his mother interrupted. "What I don't know is what you said or did that makes Chessie think that of you. Care to enlighten me?"

Telling the story of Larry and Peter Pan only took two minutes, but Diggy had to struggle over his quarrel with Chessie. His mother had a slight smile at the corner of her mouth as she listened. Nothing she heard about Chessie's outburst seemed to surprise her.

"Then," Diggy ended, "she insults me by calling me a philistine. Just because I wouldn't buy that stuff about Larry and Pat Pen."

"Who is Pat Pen? I thought you said Larry's unseen friend called herself 'Peter Pan'?"

Diggy looked at his mother in surprise. "Did I say 'Pat Pen'? Sorry, I meant 'Peter Pan.'" He put the salad bowl on the tray and fumbled with the silverware.

"I think," his mother said softly, "that Chessie is right. Larry is a romantic and is trying to help a fair maiden in danger. So that makes two known romantics in the Galaxy Gang."

"Two? Who's the other one?"

"Chessie—and guess who her knight in shining armor is?" Mrs. Caldwell laughed as her son fled from the kitchen, his face red.

Diggy would not allow himself to believe that Chessie had romantic notions about anyone, much less Diggy Caldwell. That sort of thing would destroy the gang faster than a bomb. He had seen it before. The Knights had been a great gang—lots of fun, until the head guy and one of the girls started going out together. After that it was bickering, fighting, jealousy, all over the place. No, thanks, Diggy thought, that's not for me. Mom better be wrong or the gang is in trouble.

Pat Pen. What kind of slip was that? The name bugged him. Pat Pending? Why should he be thinking of a patent pending?

He was setting down the silverware—forks to the left, knives to the right—when it hit him. "The police are investigating the disappearance of a young woman in center city. Patricia Penndell was last seen . . ." It had been on the news and without his being aware of it, the sound of that name had made an impression on his mind. Why?

Of course, Diggy thought, it may just be a coincidence, but Pat Pen certainly sounds like Peter Pan. It was close enough so that when Diggy had wanted to say Peter Pan, the name Pat Pen had slipped out. Could this be Larry's mysterious game player? Was Larry right? This woman had certainly disappeared and the police were hunting for her.

Leaving the table setting unfinished, Diggy hurried into the living room and picked up the evening paper. The story was buried on page eight. It was only ten lines long, but by the time he had finished reading it, Diggy's heart was pounding.

Patricia Penndell, twenty-four, is the object of a police search, it was announced today by Inspector John Lloyd of the Fraud Squad. The young computer analyst was last seen leaving her apartment at 310 Green Street early Sunday morning. Her purse and one shoe were found today on a wharf at Front and Delaware. The police refuse to say why this search is being conducted by the Fraud Squad but urge anyone with information about the whereabouts of the young woman to contact Inspector Lloyd. A telephone number followed.

A young computer analyst . . . last seen Sunday morning . . . The words were burned on Diggy's brain. His hands trembled as he read the news story again and again. There was no doubt in his mind now. This could not be a coincidence.

Patricia Penndell—Pat Pen—was Peter Pan!

As Diggy raced to the hall telephone he heard his mother's angry summons to finish setting the table. "Can't," he yelled. "Something important has come up. Don't wait supper for me." He dialed Larry's number and waited, shifting from one foot to another, while the phone rang for a long time at the other end. Giving up, he dialed Sphinx. "Osgood residence," a stilted voice with an English accent answered. "This is Montague, the butler. Kindly state your business in as few words as possible."

"Sphinx!" Diggy shouted. "Cut the act. Something has happened. Meet me in the lobby right away." He slammed down the receiver and was out the door before his mother could protest. Page eight was still clutched in his hand and behind him the rest of the evening paper littered the hallway floor.

Sphinx had raced down ten flights of stairs and was waiting in the lobby when Diggy came out of the elevators. Without a word, Diggy thrust the newspaper into Sphinx's hands. Sphinx peered at it and began to read aloud. "The City Council began debate today on the latest . . ."

"Not that one! This story—here at the bottom." Sphinx pushed his glasses back and read the story. Then he whistled softly.

"Yeh, Dig, I see what you mean. This could be Larry's girl friend."

"Could be? It has to be or it's the biggest coincidence of all time. Don't you get it? Patricia Penndell —Pat Pen—Peter Pan. I'll bet that was her nickname in school."

Sphinx nodded. "We have to find out if she worked for a stockbroker. That will be the clincher," he said.

"I tried to call Larry, but he's not home."

"Of course not. This is Friday night. Where would a rabbi's son be but in the synagogue with his family?"

Diggy groaned. "Stupid of me. And we can't disturb him until tomorrow night when the Sabbath ends. What do we do?"

Sphinx grinned. He had heard of the quarrel between Diggy and Chessie and he secretly relished his next words. "You have to persuade Chessie to go to Sergeant Gauss and find out more about this case. Now, come on, Dig, don't look so upset. You know that Chessie is the only one who can sweet-talk the sergeant into telling us anything. He's a good friend of Mr. Morelli's. I think they belong to the same lodge—The Exalted Order of Something Something Something."

"She'll never do it," Diggy said miserably. "She hates me." Then he remembered what his mother had said, and blushed.

"You've got to try," Sphinx insisted. "It's for Larry, y'know. Here's a chance for us to show how we feel about him. If Chessie kills you, it will be in the line of duty. Okay?"

"Why do I have the feeling that you're enjoying this whole thing?" Diggy grumbled. "Why don't you ask her? You can say that you spotted the news story."

Sphinx recoiled. "What, tell a lie! You're asking me to deceive one good friend and deprive another of glory? Never! An Osgood would never sink so low."

"Okay, okay," Diggy conceded, "far be it from me to ask you to break the code of the Osgoods—which must include the duty to stuff their faces with everything in sight that is edible. I'll give Chessie a call in the morning and go see her."

"Call her tonight and give her a chance to prepare her trembling heart for a visit from her . . ." Sphinx ducked under Diggy's swing and fled to the elevators.

3

□ The officers assigned to the Tenth Precinct police station paid no attention to the two teenagers sitting on the bench near the entrance. Young people were not an unfamiliar sight at the station. Every day they came in to complain about a stolen bike or having their lunch money ripped off by a school hustler. Then there were those who came in guarded by an arresting officer: some defiant and some in tears. Only the charges were different—shoplifting most of the time but once in a while something much more serious.

The desk sergeant who had greeted them suspiciously when they asked for Sergeant Gauss watched them as they waited. They did not look as if they were in trouble or were here to complain, but you never know. Teenagers spelled trouble one way or another. As the father of three potential troublemakers, the desk sergeant was sure of his grounds.

The girl was pretty, he noticed, long black hair and an olive skin. The boy was of medium height, husky, with wheat-colored hair and a strong jaw. They didn't seem to be on very friendly terms, judging by the stiff way they sat there, ignoring each other. I hope Gauss knows these two and wants to see them or he'll tear my head off, he thought.

When Chessie answered Diggy's telephone call the night before, her voice had been cold and unfriendly. Only after she had been told of the disappearance of Patricia Penndell and the probability that she was Larry's Peter Pan did the icy edge vanish. She had agreed to talk to Sergeant Gauss and told Diggy to meet her in front of the Tenth Precinct station at nine o'clock the next morning.

Afraid to be late, Diggy had arrived twenty minutes early. Chessie swung around the corner, ignored Diggy, and walked into the police station, her head high. Sheepishly, Diggy had followed. The desk sergeant had been treated to Chessie's sweet-talking routine and against his better judgment had agreed to let the two teenagers wait until the sergeant returned. "It may be a while," he warned.

By Diggy's watch, it was forty-eight minutes before a short, heavyset man with thick eyebrows and a broken nose walked into the station. His hair was grayer and there were a few more wrinkles on his ruddy face, but Sergeant Marty Gauss still walked with a firm tread and dominated the large room. Following the desk sergeant's pointed finger, he spotted the two teenagers and his lips tightened. Diggy could swear that he heard a groan even in that noisy room.

Without a word, Gauss pointed up the stairs and the two youngsters followed him to the second-floor squad room. Once behind his desk, the sergeant leaned back in his chair and stared at his visitors.

"Francesca," he said in a voice that was surprisingly soft for such a big man, "I wish that I could say that I am delighted to see you. I wish I could believe that you have come just to say hello to an old friend, maybe with an invitation to dinner from your parents, or with some of your chocolate chip cookies. Well, I saw your father yesterday and nothing was said about dinner and I don't see a package, so I ask myself, what could it be? Also I note the presence at your side of one Digby Caldwell. From past experience, I smell trouble—Galaxy Gang trouble. Now, please, tell me I'm wrong and this is just a friendly visit."

"*Sergente,*" Chessie responded sweetly, "we are here as good citizens to do our duty by aiding the police in their work." Gauss moaned and buried his head in his hands.

"We have information about the disappearance of Patricia Penndell," Diggy offered. The sergeant's head snapped up. He leaned back in his chair and said, "What information?" As Diggy told the story Gauss listened intently, tapping a pencil against his

33

palm. He interrupted only once, to ask if Larry had ever met or seen Peter Pan. When Diggy admitted that no one had, the sergeant merely grunted.

When Diggy finished, Gauss said, "Okay, so what have we got here? Your friend Larry is playing some computer game with a girl he's never seen who calls herself Peter Pan. This girl cuts off in the middle of the game saying something has frightened her. What probably scared her was her boss coming in and finding her using his expensive computer to play games with some thirteen-year-old . . . What do they call these computer nuts?"

"Hackers," Diggy said.

"Nerds," Chessie put in.

"Okay," Gauss continued, "so the boss sends her out of the office and probably suspends her for running up the bill for electricity and the telephone. He's smart enough to have the telephone number changed so no more nerds would be calling—that's why the operator said it was disconnected. And Patricia Penndell doesn't sound like Peter Pan to me. I think you kids have an overactive imagination and got all excited about nothing."

"What about this?" Diggy said. "We know that Peter Pan works for a stockbroker. Now, the newspapers didn't say where Patricia Penndell worked, but if she worked for a stockbroker . . . ?"

"It ain't my case, kid."

"No," Chessie said, "but you know the officers who are working on this case, don't you, *sergente?*"

The sergeant reached for the telephone. "Here I go making a laughingstock of myself with the boys downtown. I'm sure they'll be delighted to know that teenage investigators are working on this case. Wait till I tell them your theory about 'Peter Pan.' That's what I call real evidence." He dialed a number. "This is Gauss, Tenth Precinct. Let me talk to Inspector Lloyd in Fraud."

It took a few minutes to get the inspector on the phone. Finally the sergeant said, "Inspector, this is Sergeant Marty Gauss, Tenth Precinct. About this Penndell case, I have a witness here who says he was in touch with her on Sunday. He's not sure because she used a code name. Yeah, a code name—Peter Pan. Look, Inspector, I know it sounds crazy . . . yes, sir, I know how busy you are. We're all pretty busy these days. Well, can you just tell me where this Penndell worked? Yes, I see. Thank you, sir." When Gauss hung up, there were beads of perspiration on his forehead. He glared across the desk.

"Francesca, you're sure you don't know anyone else on the force who can help you with your problems? Okay, kiddies, the girl worked for a big stockbroker firm in center city. So what? Do you know how many women work for stockbrokers in a city this size?"

"How many," Diggy demanded, "are computer analysts, send out a call for help, and then disappear?"

Gauss shook his head and grumbled, "You don't

know that. You're just guessing." He leaned over the desk and shook a finger at them. "Now, I'm warning you. Stay out of this case! The inspector is a tired, overworked man who will *not* be overjoyed to find the Galaxy Gang underfoot while he investigates what happened to this Penndell woman. Francesca, don't make me go to your father. Caldwell, be smart for once. This thing is too big for you kids to mess in." He waved away their mumbled good-byes. As they left the squad room the two teenagers looked back and saw the sergeant deep in conversation with another detective. Gauss seemed to be giving orders.

Outside the station house, Diggy and Chessie strolled down Pine Street, comparing notes. They agreed that there was little reason to be optimistic about getting the police to help them. "I think we've tried his patience just a little too much in the past," Chessie remarked. "He growls every time he hears someone say 'Galaxy Gang.'" Then she realized that she had slipped back into her old friendly relationship with Diggy. "Not that you haven't given him reason to be suspicious of us," she snapped, but it was too late. Diggy knew that the crisis had passed.

They walked in silence for a while. Finally Diggy said, "Let's meet in the clubhouse tonight at eight. I'll call the others, okay? We have a lot to talk over."

Since Judge Jarrell no longer owned a car, his garage was used as a clubhouse and to store a few pieces of old furniture. A little after eight o'clock the Galaxy Gang sprawled on the dusty sofa, in two deep armchairs, a red plush love seat, and a reclining desk chair with a torn back. The only light was a bare bulb overhead.

When Larry came running in, he was panting with excitement. Even in the telephone conversation with Diggy he had kept up a rapid flow of "I knew it . . . it has to be her . . . I was right, Dig, wasn't I?" All the pain and disappointment of the last week was forgotten. As he dropped heavily into the love seat with Chessie, she tried to calm him.

Sphinx rolled the desk chair around to face the others and began. "Let's get started," he said. "You all know the story—Diggy and Chessie got nowhere with the police. They don't believe Larry's story and they don't believe that Peter Pan is Patricia Penndell. Is there anybody here who doubts that they are one and the same?"

"I believe Larry," Bobbie said hesitantly, "and I'm almost positive this is the right girl, but we have to prove it. We have to be absolutely sure. If it's a mistake, we can be in big trouble."

"So how do we prove this is the same girl that Larry knows as Peter Pan?" Diggy's voice was uncertain.

Larry sat bolt upright and shouted, "Andy Willis! Andy Willis has seen Peter Pan!" Everyone stared as he bounced up and down in the love seat. "Who's Andy Willis?" five voices asked.

"Gosh, I'm sorry," Larry said, "I should have told you before. Andy Willis owns a computer store where all the hackers hang out. He's seen Peter Pan twice and talked to her."

"Great," said Sphinx. "Now all we need is a recent photo of Pat Penndell and we're in business. If this Willis guy says this is Peter Pan, well, that's all the proof we need. Right, Bobbie?" Bobbie nodded.

"And Pat Penndell lives at . . . ?" Sphinx pointed to Diggy, who dug the newspaper article out of his jacket pocket.

"At 310 Green Street. In an apartment house."

Tilo spoke for the first time. "Isn't it strange that the newspaper didn't carry a picture? If the police are looking for this woman, surely they would want her picture in the paper."

"Good point," Sphinx said. "Maybe there are no photos of her."

Bobbie shook her head. "Everybody's got photos— snapshots on vacation, birthday parties, driver's licenses, passports . . . you can't escape them."

"Unless," Chessie said thoughtfully, "you deliberately went out of your way to avoid having your picture taken, and destroyed all the ones you had."

"Why would she do that?" Tilo asked. Chessie shrugged.

"Okay, okay," Sphinx said, "so someone has to go to 310 Green and see what they can find out from the neighbors. You can be sure that Sergeant Gauss has passed the word around to watch out for Dig and

Chessie, so it had better be Bobbie and me. There might be a policeman guarding the apartment. Don't worry, Tilo, you'll get your chance later."

"What about me?" Larry asked. "Why am I being left out?"

"We're saving you," Sphinx told him. "You're the only one who knows Andy Willis, and it's better if the police don't spot you nosing around and asking questions. What do you say, Bobbie, tomorrow around eleven?"

"Yeah, okay."

As they left the garage and headed home, Diggy cocked his thumb at the nearby house and asked, "I wonder what the judge would say if he knew what was going on."

"Simple," Bobbie replied, "he'd say *'Stop!'*—and he'd probably be right."

Third and Green was in an old neighborhood on the edge of the new Society Hill. In a few years it would become fashionable and the developers would move in, tear down the narrow three-story brick row houses (most of which had been built before World War II), and put up the modern glass-concrete-and-aluminum boxes favored by rising young executives. Until that happened, the area would continue to decay quietly with a certain grace despite the grime-darkened walls and the littered streets.

"Like an old duchess," Bobbie observed, "fallen on

39

hard times. Her beauty is gone forever and she has to pinch pennies while living in a one-room shack."

The apartment house at 310 Green was surprisingly well kept and recently painted, the two small plots of ground in front filled with flowers and the lobby scrubbed and clean. There was no doorman and no elevator for the three-story building. Sphinx checked the twelve mailboxes just inside the entrance.

"Here it is," he said. "P. Penndell. Apartment 3-B. Wouldn't you know that she'd live on the top floor?"

They climbed the stairs. There was no one in the hallway on the third floor. If there had been a police guard in front of 3-B, he was gone. "He may still be in the apartment," Bobbie whispered. "Go listen at the door and maybe you'll hear him moving around."

"Why me?" Sphinx protested. Bobbie held her fist under his nose. Sphinx tiptoed down the hallway and pressed his ear against the door of 3-B.

"What are you supposed to be?" a young, high-pitched voice demanded. Sphinx jumped away from the door. Red-faced, he turned to face his accuser. In the doorway across the hall a freckled boy with a mass of unruly brown hair peered out at him. "What're ya doin'?" the boy asked.

Sphinx smiled nervously. "Hi. My name is Oliver and I'm a friend of Pat's. I was wondering if she was home." He pointed to Bobbie hurrying up from the stairwell. "And this is Bobbie. She's a friend of Pat's too."

The door of 3-D opened fully and the barefooted youngster clad in overalls and holding a half-eaten apple stepped out. Ignoring Bobbie, he walked over to the stairwell and peered down. Then he came back and stared fixedly at Sphinx. It was as if he was trying to memorize his face.

"Pat don't have no friends," the boy said firmly. "No one ever comes to visit her."

"Well, I didn't mean that *I* was a friend," Sphinx said uncomfortably. "You can see that I'm too young, but my mother works with her—in the stockbroker's office—and she was worried . . ."

"Why didn't she come herself if she's so worried?" the junior detective demanded. Then he took a big bite of his apple without looking away from Sphinx's face.

Sphinx glanced at Bobbie, who refused to meet his eye. "Well, you see . . ." Sphinx muttered, "my kid sister's sick . . . chicken pox, and she had to stay home and take care of her."

"What's your name?" Bobbie asked. The boy transferred his disbelieving stare from Sphinx and considered the question. Obviously he did not think that it committed him to anything, for he answered, "Barney. Barney Rickles."

"Well, Barney, this guy doesn't have a sister and his mother doesn't work with Pat. He's just making up this story to fool you."

Barney spat an apple seed close to Sphinx's sneaker and waited.

41

"I can see that you're too smart to be fooled by such a stupid story," Bobbie continued. "How old are you?"

"Ten."

"Well, here's the truth. Sphinx and I—"

"Sphinx? This guy is an Egyptian statue?"

"His name is Oliver, but who'd want to be called that?"

"Yeah, I know what you mean. My name is Titus . . . can you believe it? I call myself Barney. A Titus wouldn't last very long in this neighborhood. The gang would never let me in."

Bobbie had the handle she was looking for. "What's the name of your gang?"

"The Red Barons," the boy said proudly. "We used to be the Third Street Warriors, but that had no class, so we changed it. We just decided to let girls join . . . if you're interested."

"Look, Barney, here's the true story," Bobbie said. "One of our gang has been playing a computer game with a girl who called herself Peter Pan. The last message he had from her said that she was in trouble. He thinks that this Peter Pan is Pat Penndell. Well, the only way to prove it is to get hold of a picture of Pat and show it to someone we know who has talked to Peter Pan, you see?"

"When did this guy play the game with Pat?" Barney asked.

"A week ago," Bobbie replied. "Last Sunday."

4

□ "After I got my watch back from that little hustler," Sphinx explained, "we asked to see the letter. Barney pretended he had lost it, but I saw the greedy look in his beady eyes and offered him a dollar. Then he dug into his box and found it—just an envelope with 'Garbee-White' and an address on Broad Street."

"So we checked the phone book and sure enough, they're stockbrokers," Bobbie added.

It was Monday morning, just before first class. Sphinx and Bobbie had found Larry in his homeroom and told him the news. They had telephoned the rest of the Galaxy Gang the night before, but Larry and Tilo had been out. The other students in the homeroom looked at them with open curiosity as they huddled together, whispering. When the teacher came in and the bell rang, Sphinx and Bobbie left. They had already agreed to meet Larry in the stands of the playing field during lunch.

"Why do I always go there," Sphinx moaned. "It's cold outside."

It was cold indeed. A chilly wind blew across the playing field and scattered loose papers into the stands. Huddled together for warmth, the Galaxy Gang lost no time in settling what to do next. Larry, Chessie, and Tilo would pay a visit to Garbee-White using the old school-project ploy—"We're writing a term paper on investments"—and try to find out something about their vanished employee, Pat Penn-dell, a.k.a. Peter Pan.

They raced back to the shelter of the school just as a light rain began to fall.

Tilo had suggested that they telephone for an appointment, but Larry was afraid of being turned down. "If we're there in the office," he explained, "it would be poor public relations to refuse us. Stockbrokers worry about their image, and to kick out three students who are dying to understand how the stock market works might give them bad publicity."

The Garbee-White Company occupied the eighteenth floor of a new office building in the shadow of City Hall. As they rode the elevator, the three teenagers talked casually about recent trends in government bonds—something they had just read in the newspapers. "If interest rates keep rising," Chessie

48

insisted, "we'd better go for short-term debentures." There were amused smiles on the faces of the other occupants of the elevator and one tall, distinguished-looking man thanked them for the advice. "I'll have to talk to my broker about this," he said, laughing.

It worked just as Larry had said it would. The receptionist at Garbee-White kept shaking her head as Larry explained that they were doing a report on the stock market and the national economy—"how buying stocks and bonds keeps our factories working, that sort of thing." She wanted to refuse, but Larry would not let her get a word in. Finally she stopped his flow of words by picking up the phone. "I'll ask Mr. Prentiss," she said, "but I don't think he'll see you."

Five minutes later a stocky, round-faced young man named Dave Wilson came to escort them through the offices and to answer their questions. Some of the things they said clearly puzzled him, but he never lost his smile. He was a trainee, anxious to please Mr. Prentiss.

The main office of the firm was a very large bay area divided into dozens of little cubbyholes by low partitions. In each cubicle there was a desk, a telephone, a computer terminal, and a broker. They all seemed to be on the phone at the same time, rapidly tapping out messages on the terminals and giving information to their clients. There was a loud hum as dozens of voices repeated the latest market prices, gave advice and warnings, and repeated the orders they received. Chessie nudged Larry and pointed toward one of the terminals, but he shook his head. "No way," he whispered. "She couldn't have used one of those to play the game. They don't hook into the telephone line."

One side of the large room was taken by eight or nine private offices, "for the senior account executives," Dave explained. One door was marked RE-SEARCH AND ANALYSIS, and through the window Larry spotted a computer terminal with a telephone hookup, surrounded by racks of disks and manuals. There were some graphs on the walls that looked like forecasts of stock prices. "Who works here?" he asked.

Dave hesitated and looked around anxiously. "Uh, that's our research department. We have computer analysts trying to spot trends in the market . . . you know, what certain stocks will do over the next six months. Go up, go down, go sideways."

"That sounds great," Chessie said. "We'd like to talk to the people who do that and find out how it works." Tilo nodded and wrote something in his notebook.

"Sorry," Dave said stiffly, "but the woman who does that isn't here. She's on vacation . . . won't be back for two weeks."

Suddenly, Tilo began to shift from foot to foot and looked embarrassed. "Can you show me the way to the men's room?" he asked.

Now their escort looked around for help. "Darn,"

50

he muttered, "I'll have to get the key and show you where it is, but I can't leave the two of you here alone." He tried to attract the attention of one of the nearby brokers, but the man was on the phone and studiously avoided Dave's frantic handwaving. "Okay, I guess there's nothing for it except to trust you two to stay here quietly until we get back. It'll just be a few minutes. Here . . ." He thrust pamphlets into their hands. "Read these until we get back." Grabbing Tilo's arm, he hurried the boy toward the entrance. Tilo kept up a constant stream of apologies.

Larry waited until they were out of sight. Then he opened the door of the research office and slipped in. It took him less than ten seconds to read the number on the telephone base, pick up the receiver, listen, put the receiver back, and slip out the door. To Chessie's questioning stare, he just nodded. Despite the pounding of his heart, he was exultant. When a nearby broker looked up from his terminal, the two teenagers were immersed in reading their brochures.

So absorbed were they in the mysteries of stock transactions that they did not notice the two men who came out of one of the offices. It was only when one of them spoke that Larry and Chessie looked up. "Okay," the balding man in an ill-fitting suit said, "what are you kids up to?"

When he tried to explain about their school project, Larry stumbled over his words. Finally, Chessie cut across him and went into her soft-soap routine, complete with elfish smile and a toss of her hair. The two men were unimpressed. The bald man took them none too gently by the arms and shoved them into the office.

"Let's save ourselves a lot of time," he said. "I'm Inspector Lloyd, and you two are pains in the neck from something called the Galaxy Gang. Gauss told me about you and I had a hunch you'd show up here. I told Mr. Prentiss to call me right away if some teenagers started snooping around. I thought you said there were three of them?" he asked the other man.

Mr. Prentiss was a well-built, strong-looking man in his early forties who could have passed as an army officer. He had a rigid posture and no-nonsense air about him. "That's what the receptionist told me," he said.

"Okay, where's your pal?" Lloyd asked the teenagers.

Chessie pointed across the office to where Dave and Tilo were hurrying toward them. As they came up, Mr. Prentiss took the escort aside, whispered something in his ear, and sent him off with a slight shove. Dave fled as if from a danger zone.

"You, what's your name?" The inspector's stubby finger pointed to Larry. "Larry Strauss, sir." The teenager's voice could not have been more polite if he had been talking to the President of the United States.

"Are you the computer nut who's been flying around with Peter Pan?" Lloyd asked. Mr. Prentiss stiffened and stared at Larry. The inspector said to him, "This kid says he was playing some game with another computer buff named Peter Pan and that this Peter Pan cut off after saying she was in trouble. All this was supposed to have happened the day your girl disappears."

"How did you know she worked here?" Mr. Prentiss asked the kids.

"A friend of hers told us," Tilo replied.

"What friend?" the inspector barked. Tilo shrugged his shoulders. "I'd rather not say, sir. It might get him into trouble."

"Look, kid, when I ask you a question, you answer. I'll decide who's in trouble and who isn't. Right now you three are in a pack of trouble. Interfering with an official investigation . . . withholding evidence . . . and that's only for starters. Now, who's the friend who told you?"

Larry spoke up. "Pat Penndell's address was in the newspapers. A kid who lives there showed us an envelope with this address on it. He found it in the trash." Better not say anything about the snapshot, he thought. We're in enough trouble.

The inspector thought it over. "Maybe so, but it still sounds fishy. I suggest we all take a trip down to the station and—"

"Just a moment, Inspector," Mr. Prentiss interrupted. "I don't want to interfere, but we went to a lot of trouble to keep Garbee-White's name out of the papers. If these teenagers are taken down and booked, the reporters might get hold of the story."

Lloyd scratched his head and said reluctantly, "You're right. It might blow the whole thing. Okay, I'll let you go this time, but if I ever find any of you— and that includes the rest of your gang—meddling with this investigation, you're going to see the inside of a jail cell. Got it?"

The three teenagers nodded quickly. The idea of their parents having to come down to the police station to claim them had caused a sinking sensation in three stomachs.

"Now beat it," Lloyd grunted, "and don't let me see you again—ever!"

"I'll see them out," Mr. Prentiss said. "It's one of our rules. Escort at all times." He led the teenagers out of the office and to the elevator.

"I'm concerned about all this," he said. "Tell me, what was it that Peter Pan said to you about being frightened?"

Larry had begun to answer when he caught Chessie's look of warning. She was rubbing the left side of her mouth with her finger. It took him a split second to figure out what she meant. Peering up, he saw it: a small curved scar on the left side of Prentiss's lips. The same one that Sphinx and Bobbie had described from the photograph. Prentiss was the man with Pat Penndell on the beach!

"Nothing much," he said casually. "It sounded like

her boss had caught her using the computer without permission. Would she do that?"

Mr. Prentiss shook his head. "I wouldn't know. Research isn't my department. I suppose I saw her around, but we have a lot of young women working here. I don't think we were ever introduced." He pressed the elevator button impatiently.

And that is one big fat lie, Mr. Prentiss, Larry thought. Why would you go to all this trouble to deny knowing someone who worked here?

The elevator doors opened and, after subdued good-byes, the three teenagers got inside. Their last impression as the doors closed was that Prentiss was about to say something, but he was cut off. Another warning not to get mixed up in this business?

"What's going on?" Tilo asked. Chessie explained about the scar on Prentiss's lip and the snapshot of him with Peter Pan. "So he lied," Tilo said thoughtfully. "Why?"

"Don't know," Larry said. "And here's something else. The telephone in the research room is the one that Peter Pan used, the one the operator said was disconnected. Today it's working just fine."

The elevator stopped at the tenth floor and an elderly, well-dressed man entered. He smiled at the youngsters and began to read his newspapers. When the doors opened at the lobby floor, he got out. Larry held out his arms to keep Chessie and Tilo from leaving. "Wait," he whispered. "I've got an idea." He pressed the button marked GARAGE, the doors closed, and the elevator descended smoothly. When the doors opened again, they stepped out into the underground parking area.

Chessie looked around at the lines of parked cars in bewilderment. "What's going on, Larry?"

Larry walked rapidly across the garage to the exit, then up the slope to the crowded street. He stood staring back at the garage. "Yeah," he said at last, "this was how they did it."

"Did what?" Tilo asked.

"Got her out of the building. Did you notice the desk in the lobby? Well, there's a guard there after hours and on weekends. He didn't see Pat Penndell enter or leave that Sunday. Remember what the newspaper said? She was last seen leaving her apartment. We know she was using the computer in the research room about five P.M., and she hasn't been seen since. So if she was in danger, if they kidnapped her, how did they get her past the guard? The only way is down here—through the garage."

Chessie shook her head. "Nope, Larry. What's the point of putting a guard in the lobby if anyone can sneak in through the garage and take the elevator up? This place must be guarded too, after hours."

Larry groaned and slapped his head. "You're right, Chess. I must be getting stupid."

"Also," Tilo added, "how did she get into the building without the guard seeing her? She may call herself Peter Pan, but she can't fly up eighteen stories, right?"

Larry nodded. "There's no way she could have gotten in or out of the building without being seen, but we know she was there. What a mess!"

"If she was drugged and dragged down to the garage," Tilo said, "they could have shoved her into the trunk of a car and gotten her out that way."

"Which still leaves the problem of how she got in past the guard," Chessie said stubbornly.

They walked down to Pine Street, turned left, and headed for home. All they really knew was that Prentiss had lied about knowing Pat Penndell—another strange fact in what was turning out to be a very strange case indeed.

5

□ Two days passed and Larry was no closer to solving the mystery. As often as he racked his brains for an answer, he always returned to the inescapable fact that Pat Penndell had gotten into and out of a guarded office building without being seen. It was impossible—but that is what she had done. She had played the game with Larry that Sunday afternoon using the phone in the research room at Garbee-White. No mistake about that, but how was it possible? Why had Prentiss lied about knowing her?

His head spinning, Larry walked home from school on a chilly Wednesday afternoon. He was so absorbed in his own thoughts that he didn't notice the large blue sedan that had been following him since he left the school yard. In the front seat, two men watched him as he crossed the street and walked along the brick wall of the park. The car pulled ahead of Larry and stopped at the curb. The driver watched his rearview mirror for other traffic as his passenger got out and strolled over to Larry. He was wearing dark glasses and a trench coat. Later, Larry remembered wondering why anyone would be wearing sunglasses on such a cloudy day.

"Excuse me," the man said politely, "may I talk to you for a few minutes?"

At first Larry thought he was a detective from Inspector Lloyd's squad, but he did not act like a man with authority. He looks like a pet that expects to be shoved away, Larry thought. He was not the least bit afraid. He had no idea what the man wanted, but there seemed to be no threat of danger. Besides, they were on a city street with people passing all the time. "Okay," he replied.

Larry and the man walked into the park and sat on a bench near the entrance. The driver stayed in the car, never taking his eyes off the rearview mirror. He seemed fascinated by the traffic coming down the one-way street.

The stranger took a bag out of the pocket of his trench coat, opened it, and offered Larry roast peanuts. They sat for a while cracking the shells, popping the nuts into their mouths, and building up a neat pile of shells on the bench between them.

"Nice park," the stranger said finally. He waved his hand to indicate the trees, the shrubs, and the flowers. "When I was a kid, I used to walk miles to find a park like this . . . just to see something green."

Larry threw a peanut high in the air and tried to catch it in his mouth. It bounced off his forehead onto the gravel path, where an alert pigeon waddled over and swallowed it.

The man was about forty, a little heavy and slightly bald. He seemed to have trouble breathing, and when he started to talk, there were pauses between every two or three sentences while he caught his breath. He carefully put all the peanut shells back in the bag before he spoke.

"Okay, here's the story. I work for a very important man. Because he's a good businessman, he invests his money in stocks and bonds and so on. Make your money grow, he always says. But that means that a lot of other people are handling your money for you. You know what I mean, Larry?"

Larry nodded without answering. How did the man know his name?

"The problem is always the same: greed. People start figuring the angles—how they can get a lot of money without getting caught." A young woman came jogging down the path and the man stopped, waiting until she went past. "So what we'd like to know, Larry, is this. Where is Pat Penndell?"

"What makes you think she took the money?" Larry asked hotly.

"I didn't say she did, did I? You see, Pat Penndell is a whiz with computers—so maybe she can tell us

how somebody can get past the security on a particu-
lar account and transfer all the money in that account
to . . . well, we don't know where. People who
know about these things say it can't be done, but
somebody did it, all right."

"Why doesn't this big boss of yours go to the police?" Larry asked.

"Well, my boss doesn't like to bother the police.
Let's just say that he's a very public-minded citizen
and he knows how busy they are with all the mug-
gings and holdups. No, he wants to find out for himself where the money went. If he can get it back, he'll
forget the whole thing. No harm done." The man
stared down at Larry as if the teenager was about to
produce a stack of money from the pocket of his
windbreaker and end the whole unpleasant affair.

And his boss doesn't want the police to ask too
many questions about where the money came from,
Larry thought. What do they call that . . . a "laun-
dering" operation? Money gotten from some crime is
put into the stock market to buy stocks and bonds,
then later these stocks and bonds are cashed in for
fresh untainted money. So somebody had gotten into
Mr. Big's account at Garbee-White and emptied it.
Larry knew it couldn't be Pat Penndell. Just because
she knew computers didn't make her a criminal.

"We just want to ask her some questions," the man
said.

"What makes you think I know where she is?"

Larry asked. "And how do you know who I am, any-way?"

The man pursed his lips and stared up at the sky. "Let's just say that a certain friend of ours works in a broker's office—"

"Why don't we call it Garbee-White?" Larry interrupted.

"This friend happens to hear you and two other kids talking to a certain police inspector. Pretty clever the way you figured out that Peter Pan was Penndell. By the way, we talked to the Rickles kid. Cost us a fortune before he even admitted he knew you. Said you asked a lot of stupid questions, then went away."

Good for Barney! Larry thought triumphantly. He didn't say anything about the snapshot, so this guy doesn't know anything about Prentiss and Pat Penndell. Well, he's certainly not going to get it out of me.

"We thought Pat Penndell might have been in touch with you since she disappeared."

"What about the shoe and the purse they found on the wharf?"

The man shook his head. "Kid, when you get hold of this much money, you don't end it all in the river."

"Maybe she didn't jump in the river. Maybe someone pushed her." Larry's voice broke as he pictured the water-soaked body slowly floating down the Delaware River and out into the Atlantic.

"We don't think so. Why leave a shoe and a purse

behind? But you're not answering my question. Has Pat Penndell gotten in touch with you?"

Larry shook his head. "No, she hasn't. Not a word."

"Okay. We thought that you were just some kid out looking for his girl friend . . ."

"She's not my girl friend. I never even met her."

". . . but the boss wanted me to talk to you anyway. If she does call, tell her to telephone this number for a proposition that might interest her very much. I'm not asking you to tell us where she is. Just give her my message and this phone number." He handed Larry a slip of paper.

There was a loud blast from a car horn. They stood up and walked toward the entrance. "Larry," the man said, "don't get mixed up in this thing. It's not as simple as you think." He dropped the bag of empty shells into the trash can and walked to his car. Across the street a police cruiser was passing slowly. The man got into the car and it quickly pulled away. The squad car waited a moment, then followed.

A lot of confused questions were swirling in Larry's mind. Was Peter Pan a thief? Did she rob some gangster's account at Garbee-White, fake a suicide, and disappear with the money? How did she get in and out of the building that Sunday? What part did Prentiss play in all of this? Why was that guy—"Mr. Peanut," Larry had dubbed him—so sure that Pat Penndell had not ended up dead in the river?

And now the Galaxy Gang had *three* warnings not

to concern itself with the disappearance of Pat Penndell: one from Sergeant Gauss, one from Inspector Lloyd, and now one from some gangster. Without realizing it, Larry's pace quickened until he was almost running. He did not slow down until he reached home.

"Gosh, Larry, it sure sounds like the Mafia." Diggy's voice was loud with excitement. Larry winced and held the telephone receiver away from his ear.

"The funny thing is that the guy seemed so nice. Does that sound like a Mafia hit man to you?"

"Nope."

"So now we know that a gangster had a lot of money in an account at Garbee-White. Someone got through the security codes and transferred the money out—and Mr. Big wants his money back. Remember what Mr. Peanut said: 'No harm done.'" Larry was indignant as he continued, "And they think Pat Penndell stole it!"

"Well, she disappeared, didn't she? And she was a computer programmer, so she could probably figure out how to get into all those accounts. It looks bad for her."

"I don't care what anyone says," Larry shouted. Now it was Diggy's turn to move the receiver from his ear. "She couldn't have done it. Maybe somebody tricked her into writing a program to get past the security code, robbed the account, and then—" He stopped suddenly.

"Yes," Diggy said, "it could have happened that way. What do we do now?"

"Well, the only clue we have is that Prentiss knew Pat and lied about it. Maybe he's the guy behind this. Suppose we put some pressure on him—let him know that someone knows he's lying. Drip, drip, drip, the Chinese water-drop torture, remember?"

"Gee, Larry, I don't know. This Prentiss strikes me as pretty tough. Do you think it will work?"

"Got a better idea?"

"No," Diggy said, "but this has to be talked over with the whole gang. Remember what Sergeant Gauss said about making threatening phone calls?" They agreed to present the scheme during lunch period tomorrow. After they hung up, Larry sat trying to figure out how the others would react to his plan. Tilo would support him out of loyalty. Larry had brought the Vietnamese boy into the gang and they were best friends. Chessie would probably agree. Bobbie would object to going after Prentiss without any proof that he was involved in either the robbery or Peter Pan's disappearance. But it was Sphinx who worried Larry most.

Later that evening he was still thinking through his arguments to convince Sphinx that his plan was logical and even inevitable, when the phone rang. His parents were out, so Larry picked up the receiver. "Hello?"

"Lawrence." The voice was cold and formal. "This is Judge Jarrell. Please be in my study tomorrow at four o'clock sharp. You will bring the other members of the so-called Galaxy Gang with you. There will be no excuses for failure to attend." There was a click as the judge hung up.

Mrs. Emily, the judge's elderly housekeeper and cook, opened the door at Diggy's first knock. One by one, six nervous teenagers filed past her into the long, dark hallway. Closing the door, Mrs. Emily waved them into the study by fluttering her apron, like a mother hen with a brood of chicks. She pointed to the six kitchen chairs lined up in front of the mahogany desk, then silently withdrew. The heavy door closed with an ominous bang.

They sat down without speaking. Larry crossed his arms defiantly on his chest and tightened his lips. The silence was oppressive, but no one felt like talking.

The judge's study was familiar to them. They had frequently come here for advice. Judge Jarrell had retired from the bench five years ago after a long and distinguished career. A widower, he lived alone in the colonial brick house on Fitzwater Street. Mrs. Emily took care of him and the house, leaving the judge free to work on his book, a history of law in the United States. The teenagers peered fearfully at the well-filled bookshelves, wondering which of the thick volumes described the offense they had committed.

Five tension-packed minutes passed in awesome silence. Then the door opened and Judge Thomas Jarrell stalked in. The gang stood respectfully, as if some invisible bailiff had called, "Oyez, oyez, all rise," and remained standing until the judge was seated behind his large desk. With a slight flick of the hand, he motioned them to sit down.

The only sign of the judge's seventy-two years was the thinning white hair and a few deep wrinkles on his ruddy face. Sitting erect, even stiff, he looked at the "plaintiffs" with clear blue eyes that usually shone with good humor. Now they were grave and disapproving. He tapped the desk lightly with the tips of his fingers.

"You young people," he began, "have in the past ignored my warnings. I shudder when I think how close you've come to breaking the law. I don't intend to recite a long list of your transgressions, such as making threatening telephone calls and entering a factory at night . . . and possibly some other things that fortunately I never heard of. No, the present situation is bad enough." He paused and waited, but the gang had nothing to say. Tap, tap, tap . . . the long, slender fingers beat a solemn tattoo on the desktop.

"I had a very long and unpleasant telephone conversation with Sergeant Gauss. It seems that this time you six have interfered in the most flagrant way with a police investigation. Not only that, but you're guilty of withholding evidence." He glared at each of them in turn. "Withholding evidence in a criminal case is a felony, by the way—the most serious category of indictable offenses."

"Sir," Tilo said timidly, "I'm sorry, but I don't know what the word 'indictable' means."

"Neither do I," muttered Diggy.

"It means that the offender can be charged with a crime, tried, and, if convicted, sent to prison. Don't think that your youth is any defense," the judge barked. "You'll be tried in Juvenile Court, and the prison could be a reform school, but that won't be much consolation. I called you here to give you a warning, and to help you decide what to do to repair the damage you've done."

"Judge," Sphinx said. "You're acting as our lawyer, right? So anything we say to you is privileged and can't be told to anyone else without our consent?"

"I'm your friend and advisor, not your lawyer. Although I've retired from the bench, I'm still a member in good standing of the bar. Anything you say to me that's relevant to a police investigation will be taken instantly to the proper authorities. Is that clear? I know your parents are both lawyers. Well, believe me, they would say the same thing to you if they thought you were withholding evidence."

Sphinx nodded glumly and slumped in his chair. "Now," the judge went on, "I want to know everything, repeat *everything*, you know about the disappearance of this young woman called"—he consulted a sheet of paper on the desk—"Patricia Penndell."

"It's my fault," Larry said. "The gang was just trying to help me because I was down in the dumps about Peter Pan. That was the name that she used when we were playing the game and it was a while before we found out that it was really the same girl and then we learned that . . ."

"Slowly, Larry, a bit slower, please."

Larry explained how all the hackers had found a trivia game to play on their computers and how they all took code names—the judge smiled faintly at "Moby Disk." How telephone numbers were left on the bulletin board at Hackers' Heaven so that the players could find one another. He told of the early trivia games he had played with Peter Pan and how much he had enjoyed them. Then he described the last game.

"She was in trouble," Larry said, "real danger. She heard something and went to see what it was. Then she came back and typed 'I'm scared. Help me.' "

"Scared of what?" the judge asked. "Did she say what frightened her?"

"She didn't have time, I guess. After that, there were only the words 'It's on the d . . .' "

" 'On the d . . .' " the judge mused. "On the desk?"

"I think what she wanted to say was 'on the disk.' She had put something on the magnetic tape disks we use to program things into the computer or to take things off the computer for future use. She had bought a box of new tapes the day before she disappeared. But when I looked in the research room, there were boxes and boxes of unused tapes on the shelf. What I can't figure out is why she needed more."

"Maybe she didn't want to use her boss's tapes for something personal," Sphinx suggested.

Larry nodded. "Well, maybe. But I'm sure she put something important on the disk and then hid it. She was trying to tell me where it was when . . ." He stopped. "Of course she might have taken the tape out of the office and hidden it anywhere. Only she can tell us where it is now."

"No, Lawrence," Judge Jarrell said, "I'm afraid she can't." He believed in breaking bad news swiftly. "The body of a young woman was taken out of the river near Marcus Hook yesterday, just before dark. It had been in the water for some time, so identification is difficult, but the police think it's Patricia Penndell. She was murdered—shot twice in the back."

6

☐ There was silence. Death, violent death, was completely foreign to the Galaxy Gang . . . except for Tilo, who had seen what war was like.

When he continued, the judge seemed to be talking directly to a stunned Larry. "When Sergeant Gauss telephoned me and told me of your involvement, I was horrified. This is far worse than anything I could have imagined. You simply *must* stop any further interference in this case. Not only because you may hinder a police investigation, but because you—all of you—may be in danger. Do you understand? This is murder!"

Larry barely heard the judge's words. His head was spinning. Peter Pan was dead—shot dead and her body dumped into the river. His romantic dream had ended in the marshes below Marcus Hook, bobbing

among the weeds in the filthy water. He did not feel
Chessie's hand touching his arm in sympathy.

"But . . . but," Bobbie stammered, "they're not
sure it's Pat Penndell. Maybe it's someone else."

"An autopsy is being done," the judge said, his eyes
fixed on Larry. "Usually the identity can be estab-
lished by fingerprints or by the dental work. But
from her clothing, the police are almost certain who
it is. I'm very sorry."

He leaned back in his chair. "Lawrence, I don't
want to question you further, but there are some
things I have to know." Larry was staring blankly
across the desk. "A patrol car from the Tenth Precinct was passing Franklin Park yesterday about
three-thirty. The officers saw you talking to a man in
a trench coat. The sergeant had asked that someone
keep an eye on you and report back to him. When he
heard about this, he was quite upset. Now, who was
this man, and what exactly were you talking about?"

When Larry replied, his voice was so low that the
judge had to lean forward to hear him. "He didn't
give me his name. I called him Mr. Peanut because of
this bag of peanuts he was carrying." He told the
story about "Mr. Big" and the rifling of the stockbro-
kerage account, how Mr. Peanut had been anxious to
talk to Pat Penndell about the missing money, and
how he had left Larry a telephone number where he
could be reached. The judge listened gravely.

"That's about it, sir. He didn't seem threatening
and I didn't see anything wrong in just talking to

him. Besides, I thought it might help me get some information. He was sure that Pat wasn't dead—just disappeared with the money."

"Well, Lawrence, I'm afraid this Mr. Peanut isn't quite as nice as you think. Do you know what the 'numbers' racket is?"

Chessie nodded vigorously. "I'm from South Philly, and you can't grow up down there without knowing about the numbers racket. You pick a number from one to a thousand and bet on it. The winning number comes up each day from the racetrack results. If you win, you get five hundred times your bet. You can bet anything from a nickel up. Kids used to lose their school lunch money to the guys who hung around the playground taking bets."

"It's a vicious and illegal thing," Judge Jarrell said. "Larry, your Mr. Big runs the biggest numbers racket in the state and makes millions of dollars every month from nickel-and-dime bets. His problem is to hide his illegal money so that the police and the tax people can't find it and trace it to him. The stock market seems to be the way he does it. Apparently the stockbrokers aren't careful enough about asking where large sums of money come from. Well, Mr. Peanut works for Mr. Big as an enforcer, a strong-arm man, making sure that all the small fry who take the bets pay off and don't run away with the money. Sergeant Gauss told me he's called 'Shy Eddie.' "

"Well, he certainly acts shy," Larry said wryly, "as if he's afraid of offending anyone."

73

"Yeah," Chessie said, "he hits you and then apologizes. In my neighborhood we used to call them the *muscolari*—the musclemen. Step out of line, and *bam!*"

The judge smiled. "You certainly grew up in an interesting community. It's obvious that Larry hasn't had the benefit of your experience, Chessie. It might have been better for him if he had. Now, is there anything else you can tell me about this case? I think you owe it to Sergeant Gauss. Right now he's stretching a regulation or two by not telling Inspector Lloyd where he got the information about Shy Eddie and his interest in the murdered woman."

The rest of the gang looked at Larry. "We saw a snapshot of Pat Penndell and a man in her office named Mr. Prentiss," Larry said. "They were down at the seashore together."

The judge frowned. "Hardly significant, I'd say. Two people who worked together spending a day at the beach."

Six voices answered him simultaneously. "He said he didn't know her . . . he lied . . . said he never spoke to her."

"Really? That's interesting. And just how did you get hold of this photograph?"

Larry explained about Barney Rickles. "He also found an envelope with the name 'Garbee-White' on it. That's how we knew where she worked. This guy who owns a computer shop identified the woman in the snapshot as Peter Pan. And that's all we know, Judge, honestly."

"Yes. I believe you." The judge paused for a moment, his fingers once again beating a tattoo on the desktop. "You're all guilty of withholding important evidence in what is now a murder case. It's true that you didn't know how serious this was, but the law doesn't allow that as an excuse. The fact that this man Prentiss lied about knowing Pat Penndell may or may not be important. He may simply have wanted to avoid being associated with an embezzler—or he may be a married man who does not want his wife to know about his, ummm, friendship with a young woman."

"It won't happen again, Judge Jarrell," Diggy said. The others nodded.

"It shouldn't have happened at all, young man," the judge growled. "I understand your motives—but it's going to be difficult, perhaps impossible, to convince Inspector Lloyd that in a fit of teenage exuberance you happened to stumble on this evidence. He should have been questioning Prentiss days ago about his relationship with Pat Penndell. I'll do what I can. But I want your solemn promise right now that if you learn anything else about this case, you'll telephone me immediately. There is to be *no more* Galaxy Gang involvement. This is a murder case, and you six are out of it. Is that understood?"

There was a loud chorus of "Yes!" The judge dismissed them with a nod and a curt good-bye. In the dark hallway, Mrs. Emily waited to usher them out.

"The judge really gave it to you, didn't he?" she

said, laughing. The teenagers were shooed out the front door into the cold light of the street. Looking at his watch, Diggy was shocked to discover that only thirty minutes had passed since they had entered the house.

Tilo and Larry left the others at the corner and turned down Third Street. The two boys walked quickly, in silence. There were mumbled good-byes when Tilo reached his home on South Street. Larry went on, shivering as a chill wind sent papers scrambling along the pavement. A piece of newspaper wrapped itself around his leg and he hopped along, kicking it until it blew away. The canopy in front of Stern's Boutique flapped violently, then tore at one end.

"Hey, kid, over here."

With his jacket collar turned up, Larry did not hear the low summons. At the second call, he spotted the car at the curb. Mr. Peanut—or Shy Eddie—was leaning out of the car window and waving. Larry hesitated for a moment. Well, no harm in finding out what he wants, he thought. After all, nothing can happen to me in broad daylight on a crowded street. He walked over. "What do you want?" he said.

The anger in his voice seemed to startle Shy Eddie. The poker-faced driver turned his head and stared out the other window. Shy Eddie took off his sunglasses and, taking a handkerchief from his breast pocket, began to polish them slowly. The wheeze in his voice was more pronounced now.

"What's the matter, kid? I was just passing and wanted to say hello. You got something on your mind?"

Larry exploded. "Yeah, I got something on my mind! Pat Penndell! They found her in the river with two bullets in her back! And I bet your boss is responsible for killing her, right? Maybe *you* did it . . . or that guy with you . . ."

Shy Eddie put his sunglasses back on.

"Kid, you've got it all wrong. We just heard about what happened—honest. My boss would never order anything like that. He's a businessman. He runs a big business with lots of people working for him. Would he risk all that just to get even?"

Leaning forward, Larry thrust his face close to Shy Eddie and shouted, "You wanted to teach her a lesson and let others know they couldn't rip you off! Maybe you found her with the money . . . !"

Shy Eddie shook his head. "Think for a minute, kid. Why would I ask you to give her a message? Why would I give you a telephone number where she can reach me if we had already gotten the money and dumped her in the river?"

"How do you know she was killed before you gave me the number yesterday . . . unless you did it?" Larry blinked to keep back the tears. He knew that what he was doing was dangerous. If Shy Eddie had shot Pat, he would not want Larry going to the police with this story.

The driver said something and started the car. Shy

77

Eddie nodded. He leaned out the window and said, "You're wrong, kid, you've got it all backward. I guess I'll have to prove it to you when you can think clearer. So long." The two men drove away.

Larry stared after the car. I'd better tell the judge about this, he thought. He looked around for a phone booth, but there was none in sight. Across the street was Hackers' Heaven, and Andy Willis was standing out front, a broom in his hand. Larry slipped between two honking cars as he ran across the busy street.

"Nice broken-field running," Andy said. "You'd think I was having a special sale or something."

"Can I use your phone? It's important."

Andy waved him inside. "Be my guest. Just do me a favor, don't call Tokyo."

Judge Jarrell had left for the library, Mrs. Emily told Larry, and would return late. She would tell him that Larry had an urgent message for him. Yes, he would call as soon as he got home.

Larry hung up and leaned on the counter. He sneezed, and someone said, "God bless you." A stocky young man was standing at the other end of the counter, a pile of software boxes under his arm. His face looked familiar, but Larry couldn't place him. Seeing his confusion, the young man smiled and said, "Dave Wilson. I showed you around Garbee-White the other day."

"Oh, yeah, that's right. How are you?"

"Okay, thanks. I hear from Andy that you're a

whiz at these new programs," Wilson said. "Can you give me your opinion of this word-processing software? How about the Writerite?" He pointed to one of the boxes under his arm.

Pat Penndell is dead and he's worrying about software, Larry thought. Wilson went on to describe his home computer system and what he wanted to do with the new program. "I do a little free-lance writing—science fiction stories, mostly. Haven't sold anything yet, but I hope to one day. What I need is some way to . . ."

Larry barely heard him. For a man who seemed very knowledgeable about computer systems, Wilson was stumped by a simple application. It took Larry three minutes to straighten him out on what the Writerite program could and could not do.

"That's great," Wilson said. "That's exactly what I want." He handed the boxes to Andy, behind the counter. "I'll take these."

Larry tried to slip away but was stopped by Wilson's next words. "I understand that you played the game with Pat Penndell before she disappeared."

"Did you know her?" Larry asked.

Handing a credit card across the counter, Wilson said, "Yes, I saw her in the office. I'm not in research, of course, but a few of the new employees used to have lunch together once a week. She came about two months after I did. She was from California, went to college out there for a couple of years, then worked for a big aerospace outfit. Apparently she got bored and decided to come east."

"What about her family? Did she ever mention them?"

"I think her father died in a plane crash when she was a kid. Her mother remarried and moved to Europe. She said she didn't get along with her stepfather, so after college she went her own way. A real loner. We had to practically twist her arm to get her to join us at lunch."

Larry nodded.

"There was a rumor going around the office that she had been seen down at the shore with one of the top executives," Wilson continued. "I don't believe it myself. She was kind of standoffish, you know what I mean?"

Prentiss, Larry thought. Somebody saw them together. "Uh-huh," he said noncommittally.

Andy shoved the sales slip across the counter, and Wilson signed it. "Was she good at the game?" he asked.

"She beat me every time," Larry replied. As Wilson wrote his address and telephone number at the bottom of the slip, Larry glanced over and quickly memorized them.

A customer entered the store and Andy excused himself to go over to him. When Larry and he were alone, Wilson said, "You know, I feel a bit funny mentioning this, but there were other rumors going around the office, too. Apparently she had mentioned something about doing extra work—she was spending time in the computer room out of hours."

"Yeah, well, she was probably playing the game," Larry said.

"Yes, but—" Wilson glanced around as Andy came back toward them. "People were talking about *a box of disks*—something about a special program she was writing."

"What did they say?" Larry asked, grabbing Wilson's arm as he turned to go. In his mind he could see a computer screen with the green letters IT's ON THE D . . . dancing across it. "What about the disks?"

"I'm afraid that's all I know about it," Wilson said, shaking his head. "Just some office gossip. I really shouldn't be spreading it around, I guess. Sorry, Larry. So long." He hurried out of the store and got into a blue Jaguar parked at the curb.

Larry gazed after him, his head spinning. You just made one big mistake, buster! he thought grimly. Pat Penndell didn't buy those disks until Saturday, according to Andy. I spoke to her on Sunday, just before she disappeared. *When did you find out about those disks?*

7

☐ After dinner that night, Larry was still thinking about his conversation with Dave Wilson. How had he known about the disks Pat had bought? Maybe Wilson was working for Prentiss, trying to find out what Larry knew? But how did Prentiss know unless . . .

"Larry! Telephone," his mother called from downstairs.

It was Judge Jarrell. Quickly, Larry outlined the conversation with Shy Eddie.

"Thank you, Larry. I'll telephone Sergeant Gauss right away. I wish you hadn't accused that man the way you did. In the future, please try to refrain from such tactics—all right?"

"Okay, Judge."

It was only after Judge Jarrell hung up that Larry

realized he had not told him about his conversation with Dave Wilson.

Barney Rickles came home from school Friday afternoon to find Larry sitting on the front steps of his house.

"Hi, my name is Larry Strauss. You don't know me—"

"Let's keep it that way," Barney said, going around him and into the lobby.

Larry shook his head. One thing that Sphinx and Bobbie had told him about Barney was that he could be bought.

"Did you ever see a Swiss army knife?" Larry asked, pulling one of the red-handled multibladed pocket knives from his jacket. He twirled it slowly in front of Barney's eyes. "Has everything. You could build a house with this thing."

Barney hooked his fingers in his belt. "So who are you?"

"You remember my two friends who asked about Pat Penndell? They were here last Sunday, and you showed them a snapshot."

"I remember. The guy called himself Sphinx and the girl was called Bobbie. Look, I gave him his watch back—"

"I know. I just want to check on something. You told him that you used to take care of the cat when Pat went away for a weekend. Is that right?"

83

"Uh-huh, but the cat's gone. My mom called the SPCA and they came for Squeakie. Boy, he sure put up a fight."

"Okay, but she had given you a key to her apartment, right? Do you still have it?"

There was a long pause. Barney had learned long ago never to give out information without getting something in return. "Maybe I do, and maybe I don't," he finally hazarded.

Like magic, the shiny knife appeared in Larry's hand. He waved it in front of Barney. "Let me in the apartment for half an hour and this is yours."

It took Barney exactly three seconds to make up his mind. "Okay, but I have to be there the whole time."

"That's fine."

As they stepped into the apartment Larry looked around in surprise. He had pictured Pat Penndell as a woman who was fond of books and music. She had answered really hard questions on writers and composers, but there were only a few books on the shelves and no stereo or records. The apartment was almost bare: a few pieces of used furniture, a desk with an old portable typewriter, plain muslin curtains, and some cheap posters. It was the apartment of someone who only expected to stay a short time, a place not worth spending a lot of money on. Barney saw the surprise in Larry's face and said quickly, "She only moved in three months ago. She didn't have time to fix it up. She kept telling me that she had ordered a lot of stuff but it hadn't come."

The books were romantic novels, the kind that were published in droves every month. Beautiful but poor heroine falls for handsome aristocrat. Moonlight in the garden, a passionate kiss. Larry had once caught Chessie reading one and he had never let her forget it. Pat Penndell, he thought in dismay, was not the kind of girl he had thought.

"What are we looking for?" Barney asked.

"A square box about this big," Larry said, holding his hands about ten inches apart. "It has an orange circle on top with the word 'Sigma.' " Right after school he had called Andy and found out what type of computer disks Pat had bought from him.

Larry started with the tiny kitchen, going through the sink drawers, the cabinets, and the mop closet. Another thing that Pat Penndell was not was tidy—everything had been thrown in helter-skelter. There was a pile of dirty dishes in the sink and dried grease in the oven. He moved into the living room. As he had suspected, the desk was not the hiding place. The drawers had been emptied of everything but a few sheets of typewriter paper, an envelope, some rubber bands, paper clips, and a pencil stub.

He was going through the clothes in the bedroom closet when he spotted a red-and-yellow beach bag shoved into the corner. Inside was a swimsuit, a towel, cosmetics, a large bottle of suntan lotion, and a square box marked SIGMA with an orange circle. Larry looked around. Barney was in the living room, checking under the furniture. Larry slipped the box under his jacket, securing it from slipping with his belt. Luckily it was thin, so it couldn't be seen. He went on with the search, looking under the bed, in the dresser, and behind the few pictures on the wall.

"Time's up," Barney said. "We'd better get out before the super gets back from the corner bar."

In the lobby, Larry handed over the Swiss army knife. Barney shoved it into his pants pocket and said sharply, "When Pat comes back, I'm gonna tell her about you. I don't know what's going on, but it's something funny, that's for sure." He backed off and ran upstairs.

Sorry, Barney, Larry thought. Pat isn't coming back.

When Larry arrived home, Sphinx was sitting in the living room.

"Hi, Larry. Ready to help me like you promised with that program for the Science Fair?"

Larry grabbed his arm and hurried him down to the basement. He explained breathlessly what he had found in Pat's apartment and showed Sphinx the box.

"Your Swiss army knife?" Sphinx groaned. "You could have bought that kid with a hamburger!" He turned the box over in his hands. "What do you think she used these disks for?"

Larry turned on his computer. "Well, we know she used these instead of the Garbee-White disks. Why? Because what she was working on had to be kept secret and all the Garbee-White disks were probably numbered and entered in a logbook. Right? Why else hide it in a beach bag in the closet?" Sphinx nodded.

There were three disks in a box meant for four, along with a mailing envelope and a pad of mailing labels. Larry put the first disk in and played both sides. Blank. The second disk was also unused. The two boys exchanged looks of surprise.

With a muttered prayer, Larry ran the third disk. Sphinx crossed his fingers and stared at the monitor screen. "Nothing!" he moaned.

"Wait," Larry said. "Let's try the other side."

The first part of the second side was also blank.

"Oh, boy," muttered Sphinx. "Come on, baby, come on!"

Suddenly a line appeared. "Look!" Larry cried. They jumped out of their chairs and leaned toward the screen.

OPERATION FORT KNOX. Then there were three lines of program instructions followed by a series of numbers and letters. After a pause, a complicated program began to appear. Hastily, Larry turned on his printer and pressed a button. The two boys sat back to wait as the printer chattered merrily.

"Fort Knox," Sphinx mused. "Where the government keeps all its gold. Kind of appropriate, don't you think?"

Larry's eyes were glued to the screen as he tried to decipher the instructions. "All I can tell for sure," he said, "is that it's got something to do with transferring a lot of items identified by these numbers from one place to another. I suppose one of the places must be Garbee-White, but the other could be anywhere."

"But isn't there some sort of record left when money is transferred?" Sphinx asked, puzzled. "Don't the brokers have to know where they're sending the money, and why?"

"That must be why it all had to be done on a Sunday. I'll bet this number here is for an account under a phony name at a stockbroker out of state. First thing Monday morning, the computer shows this transaction and the money is credited to the dummy account. Then somebody comes in, shows the right account number, takes out all the money—and disappears."

"And all the police will have is a fake signature and a description of somebody who was probably disguised. End of trail."

The printer stuttered to a halt and the room was silent. Larry tore off the printed sheets and put them in a folder. He removed the disk from the disk drive and asked Sphinx to hand him the box.

"Wait a minute. What are these little numbers here at the bottom?" Sphinx asked.

Larry looked over his shoulder at the seven-digit number carefully printed in ink along the bottom edge of the box. "Could be a telephone number," he said. He reached for the phone and dialed. The telephone at the other end rang six times before someone picked it up.

"Hello," a woman said, sounding annoyed, "Prentiss residence."

Larry hung up hastily. "I think we got Mrs. Prentiss out of the shower."

"It figures," Sphinx said. "Prentiss planned this whole thing and got Pat Penndell to do the program for him. When he got the money, he was afraid she might talk, so he . . ." His voice died away.

"Sphinx," Larry said, "our Sabbath services begin soon and I won't be able to do anything about this until tomorrow evening. Take the printout and box to Chessie. Ask her to pass them on to Sergeant Gauss. She can say she got them from me, but I want Barney Rickles kept out of it. I don't want to get him into trouble. Okay?"

"What about the judge?" Sphinx asked nervously.

"The judge would only send it along to Sergeant Gauss," Larry said. "This way is faster."

Sphinx had left and Larry was turning off the equipment when he noticed the mailing envelope and pad of labels lying on the worktable. He had taken them out of the box and had forgotten to put them back. Well, no big deal, he thought as he turned off the lights. The program disk and the telephone number—that's what will put Mr. Prentiss on the hot seat this weekend.

It was Sunday afternoon before Chessie reported back. At her summons, Diggy, Larry, and Bobbie had met her at a diner on Third Street. Seated in a booth, they had ordered quickly and then gotten down to business.

"Well," Chessie said breathlessly, "it's certainly been an exciting time in my house the last thirty-six hours. I'm only sorry that Sphinx and Tilo couldn't be here. This is a story worth listening to."

"Sphinx is grounded for all of today," Diggy said impatiently. "I was afraid to ask why. And Tilo is helping his mother move furniture. Let's get on with it, okay?"

"Well, you should have seen Sergeant Gauss's face when I handed him the folder and the box. He was so mad, he turned an incredible shade of red. I won't repeat what he said to me. Inspector Lloyd said the same kinds of things. It was pretty bad. Anyway, Prentiss was brought to the inspector's office and Sergeant Gauss was there when he was questioned. It lasted a long time. They kept hammering at him, asking him why he had lied about knowing Pat Penndell. They showed him the snapshot, the box of disks with his telephone number on it, and the program for getting into the account. What they wanted to know was how she got hold of the password. But Prentiss wouldn't say anything until he spoke to his lawyer, who took one look at all the evidence and led Prentiss into the next room. When they came back, Prentiss confessed everything."

"You mean he killed Pat?" Larry gasped.

Chessie shook her head. "No, but it seems she got

the code word out of him—by blackmail. She threatened to tell his wife about their little weekends at the seashore. Seems they'd been having an affair for about a month."

"If she was blackmailing him," Bobbie said thoughtfully, "that could be reason enough to kill her."

"What about the money?" Diggy asked. "Who ended up with all of it?" They looked at one another, puzzled.

"So far we only have Prentiss's word that that's the way it was," Larry said grimly. "Suppose he used Pat to write the program, got her to transfer the money, then killed her?"

Chessie nodded. "Yes, that's possible. Anyway, the police are holding Prentiss on a minor charge—violating his employer's trust or something—while they trace his movements that Sunday. If somebody saw him with Pat Penndell after she left the office, he's in big trouble."

"I hope they hang him," Larry said.

Chessie put her arm around him. "Easy, Larry. He may not be guilty, you know."

"No matter what she did," Larry muttered, "she didn't deserve what happened to her."

Diggy started to say something, but a glare from Chessie cut him off. Instead he stretched and said, "Well, as Judge Jarrell made so clear to us the other day, the Galaxy Gang is out of this case—for good.

Now, what do we say to the judge when Sergeant Gauss tells him about the box of disks?"

"We throw ourselves on the mercy of the court," Bobbie said wryly.

8

□ Did Prentiss do it? Did he kill Peter Pan? Was it true that she had blackmailed him? All through dinner that night, these questions and a thousand others ran through Larry's mind. He picked at his food and barely heard his parents talking to him. He tapped out a tune on his water glass with his fork until his mother asked him to stop.

Passing up dessert, he excused himself and hurried down to the basement. Dave Wilson knew something about that box of disks. In fact, the young stockbroker had gone out of his way to remind Larry about it. Wilson wanted that box found, Larry thought. Why?

In his mind's eye, Larry saw the sales slip with Wilson's address and telephone number at the bottom. Picking up the phone, he dialed the number. He had not the slightest idea why he was making this call or what he would say. Water-drop torture, he figured.

Shake him up. Scare him a little. It worked for us once before.

"Hello." The voice was cheerful and bright, and Larry hated it. When he answered, his voice was deep and rough, with pauses for breath.

"Wilson? My boss has a message for you, so listen good."

"Who is this?" Wilson was not so cheerful now. "What do you want?"

"Just listen good," Larry growled. "My boss"—deep breath—"doesn't like being ripped off by you and that girl." Wheeze. "So he says to tell you"—cough—"that you should return the money by tomorrow night." Hack, hack. "Leave it in the trunk of your car parked in front of the Italian Market"—deep breath and cough—"we'll find it. Be smart, okay?" Larry hung up quickly. Had it worked? Was Wilson frightened enough?

If Wilson's car was parked in front of the Italian Market tomorrow night, Larry would call the police to look in the trunk. If the money was there, the case was solved.

As he sat there, his eye fell on the mailing envelope and labels that had been in the box of disks. I should give those to the sergeant, he thought gloomily. Funny to think that Pat had handled those, probably just before . . . He picked up the envelope and examined it front and back. There had been four disks in the box and one was missing. So Pat must have mailed one—to whom?

He held the pad of mailing labels at an angle to the overhead light and looked at it through a strong magnifying glass. Yes, there were some barely visible impressions. When Pat had written on the top label, it had left a trace on the one underneath.

Larry took a soft lead pencil and carefully covered the impressions with light strokes. He blew the excess graphite off and peered again through the magnifier. Only a few letters were clear, one number on the second line, and one large *P* on the third. Taking a sheet of paper from his notebook, Larry copied the visible marks:

H—— BR——I-
—2 —LL–W—LL —
P—— — 1—2-

The third line was easy: Phila., Pa., and some zip code number. Larry ran upstairs and borrowed the Philadelphia zip code directory from his father's study. There were twenty-two pages listing the Philadelphia streets in alphabetical order and giving the zip codes for the house numbers. Slowly and painfully, Larry went down the list looking for a street name with ten letters, four of which were *L*'s and one a *W*. It was on the fifth page—Callowhill Street. The map in the directory showed that Callowhill Street ran east-west, north of Market Street. About a mile from here, Larry guessed. All three-digit house numbers on Callowhill had a zip of 19123, and that fit the label too. Since the house number was less than one thousand, it could not be farther west than Tenth Street.

The zip code directory went back on the bookshelf and the Philadelphia telephone directory was grabbed from the table in the hall. Now it was a question of finding someone with seven letters in their last name beginning with *BR* and living on Callowhill east of Tenth. It took Larry over thirty minutes to scan the columns. He ended with two names: Henry Broglie at 842 and an H. Brodnik at 612.

He dialed the first number and shifted impatiently as the phone rang. Finally someone said, "Hello."

"Mr. Broglie," Larry said softly, "I bring you greetings from a mutual friend, Pat Penndell."

The voice sounded genuinely annoyed. "Who? Who is this? Is this some sort of gag?"

"This is no joke. Pat asked me to collect that package she sent you two weeks ago."

"Are you nuts? I don't know a Pat Penndell. Get lost." There was a loud click. Larry waited for the dial tone, then dialed the second number. Well, that certainly doesn't sound like the right number, he thought.

This time the phone was picked up on the second ring. The voice was that of a young woman, rather flustered. "Yes?"

"Miss Brodnik. I think we have a mutual friend— Pat Penndell?"

"I'm sorry, but I don't know any Pat Parnell."

"Penndell." Larry spelled the name. "She told me that you were a good friend of hers and—"

"Look, whoever you are." The voice was cold and angry. "This isn't even an original line. Better luck with your next try, creep!"

Before she could hang up, Larry said, "Wait! She sent you a package about two weeks ago—and instructions!" There was a long pause.

"Who are you?" she asked finally.

"I'm a friend of Pat's. I know all about the computer disk she sent you and I want to help. My name is Larry Strauss."

"I don't know what this is all about," the young woman whispered. "I don't know any Pat Penndell."

"But you did receive a package from a friend about two weeks ago along with a letter telling you what to do with it, right?"

"I told you I don't know any Pat Penndell, so stop bothering me. If you call here again, I'll call the police." The connection was broken. Larry stared at the phone until the dial tone shook him out of his reverie, then hung up.

Oh, yes, you do know her, he thought angrily, and I'm going to make you admit it.

"What are you up to, Larry?" Diggy asked. The Galaxy Gang was lunching together in the school cafeteria on Monday. Through the entire meal Larry had sat without saying a word. Now he shrugged his shoulders and chewed his sandwich without enthusiasm.

Larry had said nothing to his friends about his telephone calls the night before. He was determined not to get them into more trouble with the judge. Larry knew that the gang would not let him follow up this new clue alone, and he did not want to get them involved.

"Sphinx, do you have that copy of the snapshot with you?" he asked.

Sphinx opened his notebook and showed the photo. "I don't like to leave it in my room," he said sheepishly, "in case my mother finds it." He handed it to Larry, who shoved it in his shirt pocket without looking at it.

"What's that for?" Chessie asked. "Larry, are you still looking for the killer? That's crazy. It's dangerous to try. . . ."

Larry got up and left the cafeteria without even a good-bye.

"I don't like this," Bobbie said. "He's got a funny look in his eyes. Do you think we should call the judge?"

Diggy shook his head. "What can we tell him? That Larry has a funny look in his eyes and won't talk to us? That's not much help."

"Well, I still don't like it," Bobbie said. Uneasy, the others returned to their lunch.

A little after seven that night, Larry slipped out of his house and hurried down the dark street. The Italian Market was only six blocks away. It was deserted at this time of night. The parking lot on the west side had only four cars in it. Larry stopped to look, but Dave Wilson's blue Jaguar wasn't there. He hurried away, head bent against the chilly air. When he was out of the market, he turned north toward Callowhill Street. Two or three people passed him without a glance. Several times he stopped suddenly and turned to look behind him, but no one was following him. Satisfied, he continued to number 612.

It was a red-brick apartment house that had seen better days. There was graffiti on the front and trash on the sidewalk. The mailboxes in the entryway showed that "H. Brodnik" lived in apartment 2-C. Larry pressed the call button for 3-D and waited. There was no answer. He tried 3-B.

There was a metallic squawk on the intercom. "Yeah, who is it?"

"Telegram for Louis Yoslowitz," Larry said in a deep voice. The buzzer sounded and Larry entered the lobby. He avoided the elevator and climbed the stairs to the second floor. Apartment 2-C was at the end of a shabby hall. He rang the bell.

The door opened a crack, held by the night chain. A young woman, her head wrapped in a towel, peered out. Larry held up the snapshot so she could see it. "That's Pat Penndell. Do you know her now?"

The woman stared at the photograph. The door

closed and there was the sound of the chain being taken off. Then the door opened and H. Brodnik stepped aside to let Larry enter.

She was in her early twenties, barely five feet tall, not pretty—her nose was a little too long and her face was too thin—but her eyes were sharp and intelligent. Even in a housecoat and with her hair wrapped in a towel, she was an attractive personality. Brave or reckless, Larry wondered, to let a stranger in like that.

The apartment was neat and well furnished. There were little feminine touches everywhere: chintz drapes, a vase of peonies and chrysanthemums, art posters, and some excellent reproductions of the old masters.

"So you're Larry Strauss," the young woman said. "I thought you were much older. I'm Hilda Brodnik. Sit down." Larry chose the long sofa.

"Where did you get the photograph?" Hilda asked. She pulled a chair close to the sofa and leaned forward. He caught a whiff of an expensive scent.

"A friend found it in the building where Pat lived," he told her.

"Lived? Past tense?" Hilda stiffened and her hands fell into her lap.

"She's dead," Larry said bluntly, watching her reaction. "Someone shot her two weeks ago and threw her body into the river. The police think she was involved in a robbery."

Hilda Brodnik slumped in her chair and began to

cry. "Oh, God!" Her voice was low. "Poor Annie, to end like that!" She rose, went over to the sideboard and poured herself a drink. After a moment, she asked, "Why do you call her Pat Penndell? Her name is Annie, Annie Palko."

Larry shook his head, confused. "Are you sure? Everyone knew her as Pat Penndell, at the apartment, in her office. Even the police list her under that name."

"No. Her name was Annie Rose Palko. We went to the same high school in Monroe. That's a coal-mining town north of here. Our fathers worked in the same mine, and we all went to the same church. Russian Orthodox." She fell silent.

"What kind of person was she?" Larry asked.

"She was hard to know, and didn't make many friends. Her home life was terrible. My father was bad enough, but hers was a brute—drunk most of the time, and abusive. One day Annie came to school with a black eye. A teacher wanted to call the police, but Annie begged her not to. She was afraid that her father would really punch her out later. Her mother was no help—an old country-peasant type. She told Annie that you can't tell if he loves you unless he hits you."

"Is her father still alive?"

"Yes, he's still working in the mines. I was home only last month. Her mother's alive, too. I ran into her in church, but I didn't say anything about seeing Annie here in Philadelphia. Annie had asked me not to."

"You saw Annie?" Larry said. "When was that?"

Hilda frowned as she tried to remember. "It was in the spring, middle of May, I think. I was shopping in center city when I ran into her. It had been seven years since she ran away from Monroe, two days after we graduated. I don't know where she got the money—her father never gave her a cent, but she managed to get on a bus and get out of there. No one in Monroe has heard from her since. But there she was, pretty as ever and dressed to kill. I persuaded her to have lunch. I gave her my address and telephone number, and she said something about moving to a new apartment. She said she'd be in touch with me, but she never did call. I don't think I really expected her to."

"Did she say where she was working? Or where she had been for seven years?"

Hilda shook her head. "Not a word. She was carrying an attaché case and certainly looked important. I was kind of awed, you know. And she insisted on picking up the check for lunch. Now, that's really impressive."

There was another long pause as the young woman wiped the corners of her eyes with a Kleenex. With an air of disbelief, she said, "Why am I telling all this to some kid who shows up here with a photograph? What's going on? You say that Annie is dead, murdered—but who killed her? And why?"

Quickly, Larry told her the main facts: how he had known Annie only through the computer game, how she was suspected of robbing some racketeer's brokerage account, how her body had been found, and how one of her bosses was suspected of using her and then killing her. Hilda listened gravely. Twice during the recital she whispered, "I don't believe it. Not Annie."

When he finished, Larry got to the point of his visit. "You got a package from Annie about two weeks ago, didn't you?"

Hilda nodded. "A package and a letter. It was a real surprise hearing from her after all this time. In the letter she asked me to keep the package in a safe place and not to open it. She would come and get it soon or let me know where to send it. If I hadn't heard from her by Thanksgiving, I was to open it and read the instructions inside."

"Where is the package?" Larry asked. Hilda rose and went to the bookshelves. From behind a few large volumes she took a mailing envelope and a letter. She came back and placed them on the table. "What do I do now?" she said helplessly. "If Annie is really dead, should I open it? What do you think it is, anyway?"

Larry's eyes were fixed on the package. It was just big enough to hold one computer disk.

"I think that Pat—Annie—was being used by someone to write the program for robbing the account. I think she was afraid of what might happen afterward, so she put her confession on a computer disk and mailed it to you. If everything went okay, she could get the package back and erase the disk. If not . . ." Larry stopped and looked at Hilda. "This could be her revenge."

"What should I do? I work as a secretary in a law firm. I can't afford to lose my job, but if they find out I'm mixed up in this whole business . . ." Hilda's voice died away.

Larry had his answer ready. "I have a friend, Judge Jarrell. He knows all about the law. Suppose I call him to make sure he's home, and we can go over there now and give him the package. I'm sure he'll know what to do with it."

Hilda pointed to the telephone on the sideboard. As Larry rose, the doorbell rang.

"My boyfriend," Hilda explained. "He said he might get back early from the shore." She took off the night chain and opened the door. "Hi, honey, I hoped—" The greeting ended in a gasp.

Dave Wilson pushed his way into the room and shut the door behind him.

Hilda put her hands on her hips. "Who are you?" she asked furiously. "What are you doing here? Get out of my apartment!"

"Hello, Hilda. My name is Dave Wilson. I'm a friend of Annie Palko's." Wilson held out his hand. Turning to Larry, he added, "Hi, how are you? I didn't expect to see you here."

"So—you know Pat Penndell's real name?" As Larry spoke he reached behind him, felt the edge of the table, and pushed the package onto the floor. It fell behind the chair.

Wilson laughed and walked into the apartment, unbuttoning his raincoat. "Nice place you've got here, Hilda. I like that Titian—and that's an El Greco, isn't it? Oh, yes, Annie told me all about Monroe and how she couldn't wait to get out of there. She never liked the name Palko. She got the name Patricia Penndell out of one of those romances she was always reading. She thought it would go better with her new career."

"You told me," Larry said grimly, "that you only had lunch with Annie a couple of times with other people present. How come you know so much about her?"

The young man was unruffled by Larry's tone. "Why should I tell you about Annie and me? Tell me, what right did you have to know the truth?"

"How do I know that you were Annie's friend?" Hilda asked in a cold voice. "She never mentioned anyone like you to me."

Wilson sat down on the chair and motioned to the sofa opposite. Larry and Hilda sat down cautiously. "Let's see," Wilson mused. "You met Annie by chance on Chestnut Street last May. You had been shopping in Wanamaker's. The two of you had lunch at the Sansom House, you had a cheese sandwich and Annie had a salad. You talked about Monroe and the kids you had known in high school. Most of the girls were married and you laughed about how the plainest one had married the captain of the football team.

Annie asked you not to tell anyone that you had seen her. She didn't want her parents to come looking for her—especially that drunken father of hers."

As Wilson recited the details, Hilda watched him sharply, not letting down her guard.

"I can't tell you what a shock it was when I heard of Annie's death," Wilson continued, "and I don't believe for a minute that she was mixed up in any robbery. You know she wasn't that kind of girl."

All this time Larry had been thinking furiously. Wilson must have been waiting at the Italian Market to see who came to the parking lot. And like an idiot, Larry thought, I let him spot me and follow me. One look at the nameplates downstairs and he knew who I was talking to. He could see the edge of the package sticking out from behind Wilson's chair. If he looks behind him, we're lost.

"How did you get in here without ringing?" Larry asked.

Wilson shrugged. "Someone was coming out when I arrived, so I just walked in before the door closed. I didn't want to have to explain all this over the intercom."

"Why are you here? What do you want from me?" Hilda Brodnik asked quietly.

Wilson leaned forward. "I came because of something Annie told me just before she disappeared. She said that she had sent something to you for safekeeping, and asked me to come and pick it up in case—well, in case anything happened to her."

He's lying, Larry's instincts told him. He's lying through his teeth. His eyes flickered to the door—unlocked. How could he and Hilda get Wilson out of here?

"Annie never sent me anything," Hilda was saying smoothly, her right arm draped on the back of the sofa. "Not a thing. What made you think she did?"

"Oh, come on, Hilda," Wilson said impatiently. "I could hear you and Larry talking about it through the door. Where is it?"

Involuntarily, Hilda's eyes fell to the floor. Wilson spun around and grabbed the package from behind the chair. Larry jumped to his feet, but it was too late.

"Thanks very much," Wilson said, backing off toward the door. "Thank you very much indeed."

"That's *my* property, Mr. Wilson," Hilda said sharply. "Annie sent it to me, not to you. Give it back to me!"

"No," said Wilson. "I don't think so. It's my property now."

Larry came forward. All the pieces had fallen into place in his mind. He knew he had to keep Wilson from leaving with that disk. "*You* were the one, weren't you?" Larry said. "*You killed Annie!* You were in the plot with her all along. And you know there's something about you on that disk, right? Well, even if you take it, it won't do you any good. We'll call the police and tell them the whole story."

Wilson shook his head. "Think you're so smart,

don't you?" he said. "Well, you're not going to call the police—or anybody."

Larry looked down. In Wilson's hand was a gun.

"You're not going to call anybody," Wilson said.

9

□ Hilda Brodnik screamed. Wilson swung the gun around to wave it threateningly at her.

"One more sound," he said, "and you're dead."

Hilda stopped, her face white.

"I don't want to have to do this," Wilson said, "but I'm afraid that both of you, as they say, know too much by now. And there's too much at stake."

Can I jump him? Larry thought. Get the gun away from him?

"The kid first," Wilson said. He was pale and sweating. "Turn around, kid. I don't like to see faces."

Larry backed away, his eyes fixed on Wilson's face.

"Turn around, I said!" Wilson shouted. He waved the gun. *"Turn around!"*

Larry did not move.

"Stop staring at me!" Wilson shouted, nearly hysterical. "Stop staring!" He raised the gun.

Behind him, the door burst open and two burly men came hurtling through. Wilson spun around and fired, wildly. Then the men were on top of him and he fell to the floor.

Shy Eddie wrested the gun away from Wilson and stood up almost casually. He tipped his hat at Larry. "Hiya, kid. Nice going. You got yourself involved in stuff over your head—y'know what I mean?" He cocked his thumb at Wilson, who lay flat with Shy Eddie's driver on top of him, pinning him down.

Larry suddenly found that he could not breathe. He slumped to the floor, leaning against the sofa.

"Are you all right?" Hilda asked, coming toward him. "Poor dear!"

"Gak," Larry managed to say.

Shy Eddie shook his head. "Just lucky I had an eye on you, kid, and we had other guys watching this character here—" He indicated Wilson. "We were watching everybody who had anything to do with Annie Palko. Yeah, we knew her real name," he said in response to Larry's glance. "We know a lot more than you think."

Hilda rounded on him furiously. "I don't know who you are," she said, "but why couldn't you have gotten here a little *sooner?* We were both nearly killed!"

The man laughed. "We saw Larry come up here, and we weren't too worried—I figured I could pump him for information later—until Wilson showed up too, trailing him. We had to pick the lock downstairs to get inside, and it took a little longer than we thought, that's all. Right, Irving?" His companion nodded.

"All right, Irving. I'll keep my eye on this joker. You call the police." Shy Eddie held the gun on Wilson while his companion stood up, dusted himself off neatly, and went to the phone. He spoke in a low, clipped voice, giving Hilda's name and address. When he hung up, he gave Eddie a nod. "They'll be here right away."

"Good. Come on." Between them they lifted Wilson to his feet and hustled him out the door and down the steps. Hilda and Larry followed. When they got outside, they found the three men standing on the curb. Shy Eddie was scanning the street.

"Take 'em a little while," he muttered with an annoyed wheeze. "Police are always so slow." He turned to face Wilson. "Listen, wise guy," he said. "You know what my boss doesn't like? He doesn't like stupidity. And you've been stupid from beginning to end. As soon as this became a murder rap, my boss said good-bye to his money. He'll never see it again. The only thing left was to make sure that the guy who stole it is behind bars. Here's for what you did, you—" He swung the gun and smashed it into Wilson's head. Wilson groaned and slumped in the driver's grip.

Hilda put her arm around Larry, her face pale. Shy

Eddie wheezed, opened the gun, and emptied the bullets onto the sidewalk. Just then a squad car came roaring around the corner, lights flashing.

"So long, kid, ma'am," Eddie said. He motioned to his partner, who dropped Wilson. "Make sure he's delivered properly," Eddie said, nudging Wilson's slumped form with his foot. "Plus whatever's in that package he was after."

"Thank you," Larry managed to say, and Hilda echoed him faintly. Shy Eddie nodded and the two men sprinted toward their car. It screeched away just as the squad car pulled up.

"This is the man you want," Larry said to the two police officers. He felt numb all over, but his voice was loud and clear. "This is the man who killed Pat Penndell."

"We'll never know," Sergeant Gauss said, "whether it was Wilson or Annie Palko who first got the idea of robbing the account. The disk she sent to Hilda Brodnik tells of the plan, and names Wilson as her partner, but it doesn't say whose idea it was."

The Galaxy Gang—minus Larry—and Sergeant Gauss were seated at Judge Jarrell's dining room table. It was Tuesday afternoon, the day after Wilson had been arrested. Sergeant Gauss had been waiting for them when school let out, and had given them a ride over to Fitzwater Street. Mrs. Emily had sent Larry alone into the study to face the judge, and the others into the dining room. While Gauss talked, the gang had one ear cocked to the lecture that was taking place on the other side of the study door. Every once in a while the judge's voice could be heard: "outrageous conduct" . . . "I warned you" . . . "you could easily have been killed . . ."

"This is what we've pieced together so far," Gauss went on. "Wilson and Annie Palko met in the office, just as he told Larry. What he didn't say was that he had learned about Mr. Big's account by accident— Mr. Prentiss said that Wilson must have looked in one of the folders on Prentiss's desk one day. Wilson wanted the money and he thought someone like Mr. Big wouldn't go to the police if his account was pilfered. But he couldn't write the program to get into the account himself—he didn't know enough computerese. Then along comes Annie Palko."

Mrs. Emily brought in a tray of cookies and cake. Sphinx fell on the food like a wolf, much to the disgust of the rest of the gang. "How in the world can you eat like that while Larry's being tortured in there?" Chessie asked angrily.

Sphinx shrugged. "How's it going to help Larry if I starve to death?"

"Annie Palko had just gotten a job with Garbee-White, in the research department. She was a bright girl—in a very short time she was practically running the place. Prentiss was very impressed with her, and he was unhappy in his marriage, so it was easy enough for her to get him involved in an affair. Ap-

113

parently she was really in love with Dave Wilson, who was masterminding the whole thing." Sergeant Gauss paused, looking sober. Sphinx stopped eating for a moment.

"Anyway, Annie got the security code from Prentiss, and she wrote the program and stored it on a disk. Wilson opened an account under a phony name with a suburban broker. Then they waited for the right moment. Around this time Annie must have gotten nervous. She was in love with Wilson, but I don't think she really trusted him. She put a confession on another disk and mailed it to Hilda, her only friend in Philadelphia. She figured if it worked out okay, she could always come back later and retrieve the package."

"What happened then?" Bobbie asked.

"Well, Wilson had convinced Annie that in order to keep the mob from coming after them once they stole the money, she would have to drop out of sight completely. They were going to set it up so that Prentiss would take the blame for the whole thing. She was going to hide somewhere in the country and wait for Wilson to transfer the money and come get her. First she drops the snapshot and letter with Garbee-White's address where she's sure Barney Rickles will find it, so that attention will be focused on Prentiss."

"So when Prentiss lied about knowing Annie, he just got in deeper," Tilo said.

"That's right. It was well planned. Wilson waited

until late Sunday afternoon to transfer the money. He wanted to make sure that no one would be working in the building, so there'd be no one to find out what had happened until Monday morning. By then he'd have emptied the suburban account."

"But how did Annie get into the office on Sunday," Sphinx asked, "without the guard seeing her?"

"She didn't," Gauss replied. "She was dead. Wilson picked her up early Sunday, drove her out into the country, shot her, and pushed her body in the river."

"But—but Larry talked to her that day—played the computer game with her!" Chessie said, horrified.

"No," Gauss said quietly. "That was Wilson."

There was silence around the table.

"But how did he get into the building?" Sphinx asked.

"The guard's log shows that an electrician checked in Sunday afternoon to fix some lights on the thirteenth floor. The signature in the log matches Wilson's handwriting. He had the disk with the program Annie had written. All he had to do was put it on the computer and run it. The computer was still on when Larry called. When "Mr. Chips" identified himself and asked to play the game, Wilson saw a perfect chance to confuse the time of Annie's murder, and to throw more suspicion on Prentiss, by playing the game himself—and by pretending to be interrupted in the middle, leaving a cryptic message about a *disk*. Wilson went to Annie's apartment late that night and hid the envelope and box of disks in her closet. What a cover for himself! After the box was found, with Prentiss's phone number on it, everyone would think Prentiss made Annie Palko do it. No one would think twice about Wilson. He was careful to keep his relationship with Annie a total secret."

"So when he saw Larry in the computer store," Diggy mused, "he thought it was another chance to hint about the box of disks."

"He must have thought the police were taking too long in finding the box and arresting Prentiss," Gauss said sourly.

"So after meeting him in the computer store, Larry made that call to Wilson—" Chessie said.

"—which got Wilson all upset, because Larry had somehow assembled all the pieces to fit—" said Bobbie.

"So Wilson hides out in the Italian Market and follows Larry to Hilda Brodnik's apartment," cried ,Sphinx, waving a piece of cake in the air. "And listens behind the door while they're discussing the package Annie sent her."

"It was pretty stupid of Larry," Chessie said anxiously. "No wonder the judge is chewing him out. If he suspected Wilson, why couldn't he just call the police?"

"Exactly *my* point, Francesca." Gauss heaved himself up out of his chair. He took a cookie and crushed it in his fingers over the plate. "You kids want to disobey me and the judge? Well, then you get what's coming to you. That's the way the cookie crumbles—get it?"

Sphinx stared in dismay at the plate. "A perfectly good cookie—wasted!"

"I have to get back to the station house. May I just say, I hope I never see any of you in the line of duty again. Good-bye, Mrs. Emily," Gauss said. They could hear the front door open and close.

"He shouldn't have been so foolish," Tilo said softly.

"Who?" asked Sphinx. "Wilson?"

"No, no—Larry. He put himself in terrible danger."

Diggy gave Chessie a sly glance. "Well, Larry's a romantic, right? He wanted to save the beautiful maiden. How could he know that the lady was in cahoots with the dragon?"

The door to the study opened, and the judge and Larry came out. Judge Jarrell looked grim and Larry was pale. The expression on the judge's face grew even grimmer when he saw the teenagers gathered around his table.

"Galaxy Gang," he barked, "I have one word to say to you: *out!*"

The teenagers stood up and scrambled for the door.

"And don't come back until you have some more respect for the law!" he roared, standing on his front step.

When they were out of earshot, Diggy turned to Larry. "Well?"

"It was pretty bad."

"How bad is pretty bad?"

"Very."

Chessie came up and put an arm around Larry's shoulders. "I'm so sorry," she said. "I'm sorry about the whole thing . . . about the judge yelling at you, about Wilson, about Peter Pan . . ."

"That's the worst," Larry said heavily. "Now that I know what she was involved in . . . the kind of person she must have been . . ." His voice trailed off.

"Don't take it to heart," Sphinx said, draping his arm around Larry's other shoulder. "There are other women in your future. Trust me. I'm an expert. Anyway, you shouldn't think about Peter Pan, or Annie Palko, or whatever you want to call her. Think about yourself—how stupid you were to get involved in this whole thing. If you're going to worry about something, worry about the fact that you're a hopeless romantic—okay?"

"It's true," said Tilo, shaking his head.

"It's true—"

"It's true—" echoed the rest of the gang.

"Well," said Larry despondently, "I have only one thing to say." He looked up and a grin spread slowly over his face. "Here it is. 'It is a foolish thing—' "

"Oh, no!" groaned Sphinx. "He's going to quote something!"

118

" 'It is a foolish thing well done,' " said Larry proudly. "Dr. Samuel Johnson."

"Okay," said Bobbie. "I think you're well on the road to recovery." Laughing, the Galaxy Gang headed home through the park.

About the Authors

MILTON DANK grew up in Philadelphia, attended the University of Pennsylvania, from which he holds a doctorate in physics, and has worked as a research physicist in the aerospace industry.

Mr. Dank has written several novels for young adult readers, including *The Dangerous Game, Game's End, Khaki Wings,* and *Red Flight Two. The Computer Caper, A UFO Has Landed, The 3-D Traitor,* and *The Treasure Code,* written in collaboration with his daughter, Gloria, are the first four books in the Galaxy Gang Mystery series.

GLORIA DANK was graduated from Princeton University with a bachelor's degree in psychology and has worked as a computer analyst.

Milton Dank and Gloria Dank live and work in suburban Philadelphia.